MASSACRE AT METZ

The T-Force Thriller Series
Book Two

Charles Whiting

SAPERE
BOOKS

MASSACRE AT METZ

Published by Sapere Books.

24 Trafalgar Road, Ilkley, LS29 8HH

saperebooks.com

ISBN: 9780854954087

PART ONE: OPERATION BREAK-IN

'I'll tell you what you're gonna do. You're gonna take that bunch of rogues you command — T-Force — penetrate Metz's defences and knock that goddam Battery out before we attack Driant again. Then by God, as soon as this rain stops, I want to be over the Moselle and on my darned way to Germany, Hardt!'

Gen George Patton to Major Hardt, CO of T-Force, October 1944.

CHAPTER 1

'Okay, General, they're coming up to the start line now, sir,' the immaculate aide with the Boston accent announced importantly.

Blood and Guts Patton, standing on the bonnet of the polished jeep, focused his glasses. The thin rain dripped from the edge of his lacquered helmet, adorned with the three oversized silver stars of a lieutenant-general.

'Where?' he barked.

'Down there in the hollow, sir, to the right of the Ars-sur-Moselle road.'

'Give it *military style*, mister!' Patton snarled threateningly.

'At two o'clock, General,' the aide corrected himself hastily. He knew the Old Man's vitriolic temper and he didn't want to be posted back to the infantry to face what the 11th Infantry dough-boys across the French valley would soon be facing. 'Have you got them now, sir?'

'Of course I've goddam well got them! What the Sam Hill do you think I am — *senile*?'

The two lead companies had halted now that they were in the open again. Well spaced-out like the trained infantry they were, they crouched in the wet grass, staring tensely at the squat outline of Fort Driant high above them. Most of them seemed to be moving their mouths, as if they were chewing gum. But the Third Army commander knew differently. After two disastrous attempts to take the Fort that week, which had left the bare slope in front of them littered with dead and wounded GIs, they weren't chewing gum — they were praying!

For a moment he swung his glasses across the shell-cratered, battle-littered slope up to the Fort, its squat outline shrouded in the October drizzle. It lay silent and sinister. There wasn't a Kraut in sight. To any casual observer the place seemed harmless, perhaps even abandoned. But Blood and Guts knew otherwise. Up there equally tense and dedicated men were waiting for the action to commence. But with a difference; they were protected by a belt of minefields and barbed wire some hundred feet deep and concrete walls nearly two yards thick. And as General Patton told himself, switching his glasses back to his own men, that was one hell of a difference!

Suddenly a red flare pushed high into the grey October sky. Around him his staff tensed. It was the signal the infantry had been waiting for. An instant later the whole of the XX Corps' artillery — nearly six hundred guns — crashed into action with a frightening, earth-shaking roar. With a hoarse exultant scream the heavy shells shot over their heads, tearing the morning calm savagely apart. Salvo after salvo followed. The first angry sighs turned swiftly into one long baleful howl, which rose and rose in elemental fury.

The trench line below the summit disappeared in an instant. The creeping barrage moved forward. Great shell holes appeared in the barbed wire belt like the work of some monstrous mole. To the left of the fort already obscured by the thick yellow smoke, there was a sudden violet flash. Perhaps a petrol dump Patton told himself. He turned his glasses to the men waiting below, their faces tinged blood-red by the flames. Already their officers were beginning to rise to their feet, whistles between their lips, eyes fixed on their wrist watches. He knew what they were telling themselves. Nobody could live through a barrage like this. But they did; they always did!

Then as suddenly as it had started, the barrage ended. Silence filled the valley, while the smoke started to drift away from the summit of the barren hill. For a moment nothing happened. It was almost as if both the attackers and the unseen defenders had been mesmerised by that terrific bombardment.

Next to Patton, Colonel Yuill, who commanded the men down below, cried impatiently, 'Move out for God's sake! Move out, willya!'

As if they had heard the impassioned plea, the officers of the lead companies blew their whistles. Patton could see their cheeks bulge abruptly. Faintly the shrill sound carried across the valley to be obscured immediately by the shouts and cheers of the infantry as they began to scramble to their feet. Behind them, the Shermans' motors burst into noisy life. With blue smoke flooding from their exhausts, they waddled through the GIs to take the lead. Automatically the infantry started to form long lines behind them, bodies tensed for the first hard thwack of lead against their soft flesh.

Somewhere a heavy German machine gun began to chatter like an angry woodpecker. The Shermans ground on. Behind them the infantry quickened their pace, eager to keep up with them and the protection of the tanks' armour. The first GI was hit. His hands fanned the air and he went down to disappear beneath the tracks of the second wave of Shermans. Tracks gleamed redly for a moment. A head, severed neatly from the squashed, pulped body, rolled away like an abandoned football. Another GI sat down, his spectacles slipping absurdly to the side of his suddenly bloody face, as if he had just slipped on a banana. A couple of aidmen, stretcher jogging up and down on their shoulders, ran over to pick him up. But before they could reach him, the GI had slumped to one side. One of the aidmen took off his helmet and, poking his rifle into the wet ground muzzle downwards, perched the helmet on its butt. The GI was dead. The advance went on.

A stomach-churning howl. Rockets, trailing angry tails of red sparks behind them, shot through the grey air. Huge gaps suddenly appeared along the first line of men. A Sherman came to a halt, one track flopping out behind it like a broken limb. Another crashed into a smoking crater, its rear sprockets churning uselessly, showering the dead and dying with mud.

'*Moaning minnies*!' Yuill cried anxiously. 'Jesus, they're throwing everything but the kitchen sink at my poor guys!'

Patton ignored the officer who had suggested Operation Thunderbolt, the week-long series of frontal attacks on Fort Driant. This was the key defensive position in the encircled French city of Metz which barred his victorious progress to Germany. His anxious gaze was fixed on the second wave of attackers. Would they keep on now? Or would they turn tail and bug out, back down the hill like their buddies had already done twice that same week?

But the Shermans steeled their resolve. The tankers gunned their engines. They waddled forward more quickly. To their right a tank 75mm cracked into action. A white bolt of glowing steel shot towards Driant. Patton recognised it immediately. A solid-shot, armour-piercing shell. With a thud, which the staff officers could hear a mile away, it hit a concrete wall. It did not penetrate, it whined off harmlessly like a golf ball; but it had its effect. It kept the advance going. The attackers were clambering awkwardly through the barbed wire. Here and there a GI got caught and frantically fought the barbs clinging to his uniform, as the mg fire stitching a deadly pattern in the wet earth came closer and closer. But already others were through. Zig-zagging between shell bursts, springing eagerly over the holes, they were pelting for the Fort itself.

'*Hot shit!*' Patton yelled enthusiastically, slapping his riding crop against a gleaming cavalry boot, 'the doughs are gonna pull it off after all!'

'I knew they would, sir,' Colonel Yuill responded, 'this time the Eleventh is not going to be stopped, *no sir!*'

A burst of machine gun fire caught the leading company commander in the stomach. As his mouth flopped open a phosphorus grenade exploded at his belt. Immediately a sheet of dazzling white flame enveloped him. In a second he was a writhing torch. A noncom pushed him out of the way brutally with the butt of his grease gun and standing there, feet apart like some cowboy gunslinger, sprayed the wall of the Fort from which the burst had come. Behind him his company commander was shrinking rapidly to the size of a pygmy in the intense heat. Now the first Sherman was grinding its way up the sloping side of the Fort. Little groups of infantry were following it. Other men — combat engineers — were poking satchel charges into the Fort's apertures at the end of long bamboo poles, like boys baiting rabbits in their warrens. Another Sherman had taken up its position thirty yards away from the Fort's main entrance. Calmly, as if he were back on the tank range at Fort Myer, the gunner began to pump shell after shell into it. It slowly started to give, though every second shot bounced off as harmlessly as if the gunner had been using tennis balls. Behind it the flamethrower operators tensed, waiting to go in with their terrible weapons, once the entrance had been breached.

Patton swung round to a happy Yuill. 'Colonel, you'd better alert your reserve battalion. They can follow up —'

He never finished the order. On the grey horizon bright yellow lights flickered alarmingly. There was a sound like the *Chicago Chief* tearing down the track at a hundred mph.

Suddenly the whole world seemed filled with that terrible sound. The first salvo of enemy fire landed right on the roof of the Fort. A mile away and his staff could feel the earth tremble beneath their feet.

Trees, planted to camouflage Fort Driant's roof, sailed into the air. The Sherman, crawling towards its concrete mass, was swept over the side like a fly swatted by some great invisible hand. The mangled remains of what a second before had been men lay like lumps of raw meat everywhere.

Patton flashed a bitter enquiring look at Colonel Koch, his Intelligence Officer.

The grey-haired Colonel shrugged. The fire from the unidentified battery had come as a complete surprise to him too.

The horizon erupted once again. The enormous shells tore the air apart. Metal struck metal with a hollow boom. The Sherman outside the main entrance rocked as if a tornado had struck it. Its gun drooped. Evil little blue flames licked at its rear. An instant later it exploded with a tremendous roar. When the smoke disappeared all that was left was one sole bogie wheel wobbling its way slowly down the slope.

Another Sherman was hit. Its turret — all ten tons of it — sailed high into the air. Behind it, the panic-stricken driver of another tried to reverse and ran full-tilt into a bunch of cowering infantry. His tracks mowed through them, flailing bloody limbs and broken bodies to both sides. The elegant aide groaned out loud and bent his head quickly.

The German defenders leapt back to their machine guns, the enemy in their sights once more. The Spandau's hissed into hysterical life. Tracer zipped towards them like flights of vicious red hornets. Some of the terrified GIs threw themselves to the ground and the watching staff officers could see the slugs striking their twitching defenceless bodies over and over again. Others tried to run for cover and were caught in mid-stride.

'My God,' the elegant aide breathed, his eyes wide with fear, it's going to be a massacre!'

'Knock it off!' Patton rasped, gripping his glasses with hands that had turned into white claws. In a moment he knew he would have to make a decision.

On the horizon the mysterious new battery fired one last salvo. It sufficed. As the shells winged their way through the burning sky, the men of the 11th Infantry broke. Flinging away their weapons, the survivors began to scramble frantically back the way they had come. Here and there an officer or a noncom tried to stop them. To no avail! Eyes wide and staring, mouths dribbling with fear, they ran by. A bareheaded top sergeant, blood dripping from a scalp wound, pulled out his .45 and fired a crazy volley into their fleeing backs. Two men fell. But the rest kept on running, the wounded hopping behind them. The top sergeant threw away his .45 in disgust. Bending, he picked up a wounded boy at his feet. Together they followed the rest.

Patton lowered his glasses, his lean face grey with rage. 'All right, Doane,' he snapped at the clay-faced aide, 'don't just stand there like a spare prick at a wedding! Get air and smoke in there to cover them, willya!'

SWOOSH! As the first dive-bomber fell out of the sky at four hundred mph and the smoke shells started to explode around the Fort, Patton slapped his riding cane against the side of his boot angrily. 'All right, Yuill,' he snapped, 'let's get the hell outa here! We'll not take Fort Driant this day.'

Yuill shook his head like a man waking up from a nightmare. 'Yes, General,' he said, his voice unreal, 'Yes.'

As the few surviving officers of the 11th Infantry formed a rough skirmish line to stop the shocked GIs getting too close to the Third Army staff, he got into the jeep next to Patton.

'Mims,' he barked at the Sergeant-driver, 'take the bastard away. *Fast!*' With the siren howling, Mims put his foot down hard. The jeep shot forward, scattering the survivors. Patton did not even notice. His mind was too full of his new defeat. Operation Thunderbolt had been a total, dismal failure.

CHAPTER 2

The house had probably once belonged to some prosperous Metz citizen, long since fled from the besieged Lorraine city. The one-time drawing room was high ceilinged with tall French windows, now shattered by the almost continuous artillery fire. Wet, heavy satin curtains hung slackly from them. The furniture, ripped open by GI looters who seemed to think that every sofa or armchair hid a fortune, was plush and overstuffed. Cracked, highly-coloured holy pictures lay everywhere in the shattered glass which littered the floor. A jagged shell hole let in the grey October fog and the raindrops which dripped with mournful persistence on to the floor. Every now and again a shell from the 105mm battery up the road exploded in the distance with a muted roar.

But the assembled staff officers of the US Third Army had neither eyes for their surroundings, nor ears for the permanent rumble of the heavies. Their whole attention was concentrated on their chief, Blood and Guts Patton, as he scowled down at the map, his lean hard face as grey and depressed as the weather itself. For what seemed an age, they stood thus like characters at the curtain of a third-rate play, frozen into absurdly melodramatic positions, the only sound Patton's heavy breathing and the dreary drip-drip of the raindrops.

Major Harry Hardt, the CO of Patton's long-range reconnaissance outfit, T-Force, stared at the Third Army Commander and thought he had never seen him so depressed in the two years he had served under him; the month-long siege of the grim northern French city, which was holding up his drive for Germany so disastrously, was obviously taking its toll. The Old Man looked every one of his sixty years.

Slowly, very slowly, General Patton raised his eyes from the map of the Metz defences and focused them on the young Major. In spite of his gloom he liked what he saw. Hardt was a younger version of himself, from the gleaming brass sabres of the Regular Cavalry on the collar of his immaculate Ike jacket down to the perfectly-tailored white whipcord breeches, enclosed in gleaming handmade riding boots. There was only one difference between the two West Pointers apart from their ages: Major Hardt's lean, harshly handsome features were marred by a completely hairless skull, a pale horrible pink and obscenely wrinkled like the skin of a very old man, the result of a run-in with a Kraut flame-thrower in North Africa two years previously. Patton shifted his gaze from the young Major's skull which had gained him the nickname — behind his back — of 'Hairless Harry' in the ranks of his élite, if irreverent, T-Force. 'Major,' he rasped, 'do you know what happened to the Third Army yesterday?'

'No sir,' Hardt lied, knowing a rhetorical question when he heard one.

'It attacked Fort Driant down there in Metz for the third time this week — and failed,' he said bitterly. 'Not only that, but the doughs ran away. *My doughboys ran away!*' He looked at the younger man reproachfully, almost as if it might be his fault.

'I see, sir,' Hardt, who had given Patton his first great victory of the campaign in France, answered noncommittally, wondering all the while what the infantry's problems had to do with his force.

'No, you don't. But you soon will, Major. Come over here to the map. I want to show you something.'

In unison, the staff officers followed the young T-Force Commander to the large map spread out over the dining room table, ready to answer the questions that their Chief could bark at them at any moment. Patton rapped his West Point class ring on the map. 'Metz,' he announced, 'covered by a network of two dozen forts, arranged in two tiers. Mostly they were built in the nineteenth century, but in the thirties the French incorporated them into the Maginot Line. In 1940 when the Krauts took them over, they kept them up and modernised the most important of them, especially the four covering the crossing points on the River Moselle. Here at Jeanne d'Arc, Plappeville, St Quentin and *Driant*,' he poked his finger at the map, as if he would have liked to have poked a hole in it at the mention of the name, his lean face cast suddenly in what he called his Number Three Scowl.

'Now as you can see, Hardt, they are located on high contours, excellent sites for preventing my doughs from crossing the Moselle in strength, advancing into Kraut-land and winning the honour of finishing this war in Berlin before that little Limey, Montgomery, goddam well gets there first!'

Hardt repressed a smile at the mention of the British Field Marshal, whom Patton hated with passion because he, Patton, felt the Britisher was out to snatch the kudos of victory from his own hands. 'Now it's darn bad enough that those forts are tremendously well armoured with deep belts of wire, elaborate trench systems *and* gun emplacements protected by ferro concrete ten lousy feet thick, without the new baby that's suddenly popped outa nowhere.'

'What's that, General?' Hardt asked.

Patton did not seem to hear his question. Instead he said, 'Now in the last month, the Third has liberated over sixteen hundred miles of French territory and eight hundred odd towns.' His Number Three Scowl disappeared for a moment to be replaced by a thin smile, which revealed his dingy, sawn-off teeth. 'Now that's a record for the history books, one without parallel, and I'm not gonna have it spoiled by being stalled like this at Metz. Okay, so they say Metz's not been taken by storm for over thirteen hundred years since Attila the Hun did it back in the fifth century. So what! Georgie Patton is as good as the old Hun any day. Isn't that right, gentlemen?' He shot a fierce glance at his staff officers. There was a low, embarrassed murmur of agreement.

'But what's to stop us neutralising those forts, once our troops have gotten into the upper storey, General?' Hardt asked hastily, seizing the chance offered him by the slight pause in the General's monologue. 'Once they are established, surely it boils down to a battle of attrition. It just depends on who's got the most staying power — the Krauts down below or our guys above?'

'Yeah,' Patton snarled. 'That's exactly the argument that Yuill sold me when he smooth-talked me into trying that goddam frontal attack on Driant. Mind you, Hardt, we might just have pulled it off yesterday if it hadn't been for that goddam new Führer Battery.'

'What sir?'

Patton nodded to his Intelligence Officer, Colonel Koch. 'You tell him, Oscar,' he said in disgust.

The former professor of military history responded at once, his tone that of an experienced lecturer. 'We've got virtually nothing, Major Hardt. Yesterday the Krauts really sprang a surprise on us with those guns, which swatted our people off Driant like so many flies. But since then, we've been doing some rapid and intensive questioning of what refugees from Metz we could find in the area. There wasn't much, but we did strike a little lucky with a French engineer who had been evacuated to Etain up the road from here.' He took off his glasses and nipped the bridge of his nose, as if he were suddenly very tired. 'According to what he knew, the Krauts took over a small fort here — *Mort d'Homme* — aptly named, don't you think? — in the summer soon after we landed in Normandy. Two whole battalions of engineers were employed to get it back into shape at the double —'

'Yeah,' Patton interrupted, 'I guess the Kraut bastards knew I would be coming this way and had already started planning to make it tough for me even then.' He sighed bitterly. 'But get on with it, Oscar.'

'Thank you, General. Okay, so according to our French friend, the Krauts put in four batteries of large guns — perhaps eight inchers — each battery to cover one of those four forts. You see what I mean, Major?'

'Yes,' Hardt responded slowly, rubbing his hand over his wrinkled scalp reflectively. 'As soon as our guys get on the roof of one of the forts, the Krauts knock them off. Hell, that kinda ball game could go on for ever, Colonel!'

'You ain't kidding,' Koch replied very un-professorially.

'But why don't we take this — er — Führer Battery out by air and with artillery?' Hardt objected.

'For two reasons,' Koch answered. 'We haven't been able to locate the damn place properly and, from what the French engineer told me yesterday, the battery seems to have some sort of retractable turrets — like in the Maginot Line — which sink deep below the earth once air attack threatens. And we know from what the fly-boys tell us about their air attacks on the Maginot, that even the British blockbuster is not much good against that kind of gun turret.'

'So what are you going to do, Colonel?' Hardt asked a little helplessly, still wondering what all this had to do with him.

'I'll tell you what you're gonna do,' Patton interrupted, as if he had been waiting impatiently all the time for this particular moment, 'you're gonna take that bunch of rogues you command, T-Force, penetrate Metz's defences and knock that goddam battery out before we attack Driant again. Then, by God, as soon as this rain stops, I want to be over the Moselle and on my darned way to Germany, Hardt!'

The Major hesitated an instant. 'Sir, I don't want to appear to be trying to get out of this assignment. After all, that is what T-Force is for, General, but half of my men are new to the outfit, straight from the reinforcement centre after the casualties we took on the bridge at Pontaubault. We're still trying to knock them into shape at Verdun. Besides, sir, if we can't even locate the place, how am I going to brief them for a mission of this kind?'

'Don't worry about the first point,' Patton answered. 'You know the Third's ripple-dipples sent you the best of the bunch as replacements last month. You got the cream. I've got faith in them, inexperienced as they may be, and you'll have to have too. As for the second point,' he smiled suddenly, showing those dingy teeth again, but there was no answering light in his faded blue eyes, 'Colonel Koch here has taken care of that, haven't you, Oscar?'

'Yessir,' Koch answered promptly. For the first time since Hardt had entered the conference room in the ruined villa, Koch's severe look vanished and his eyes twinkled behind his glasses. 'Prepare yourself for a nice little airplane ride tonight.'

'What?'

'Yep, you'll be riding high with Bright Eyes himself…'

CHAPTER 3

Bright Eyes tapped the side of the all-black A-20. 'There she is, Major,' he said in that easygoing way of his, 'my own beautiful little bird, complete with a two thousand seven hundred million candle-power Helmore GEC searchlight. The Turbinlite the British call it — they first developed it, you see, at RAF Northwood.'

Major Hardt did not see. But for a moment he contented himself with studying the careless-looking US Army Corps Captain, whom everyone at Etain Field called 'Bright Eyes' and treated with a certain kind of awe. He was in his mid-twenties, with an easy smile on his chubby boyish face, a soft woollen combat cap perched on the back of his clipped blond curls. But his eyes were quick, intelligent and very alert.

'What is this — er — Turbinlite, Captain?' he asked eventually.

'Call me "Bright Eyes", everybody else does. Come on inside and I'll show you,' He levered himself upwards into the belly of the black-painted, converted twin-engine bomber.

Hesitantly Hardt followed, a little embarrassed at having to remove his helmet and reveal his puckered skull to the grinning pilot.

'Well?' he demanded stiffly.

Bright Eyes' grin did not diminish. 'This,' he said, slapping his leather-gloved hand against the auxiliary control panel bolted to the regular instrument panel. 'Flick that switch there and you'd blind half of Etain Air Base.'

'I see that. But what is it used for?'

'Hell, the British have developed a lot of uses for it since Group Captain Helmore started working on it earlier this year. They use it for lighting up surfaced subs in the Atlantic or targets in Krautland for their night bombers. But up here in the Third Army area we've been utilising it mostly for lighting up Jerry troop concentrations at night, so that our doughs can let them have it.'

Hardt stared at the careless young pilot incredulously. 'But wouldn't that mean you'd be a sitting duck, illuminated like that by your searchlight? *I mean for Jerry flak — or night fighters?* And I hear there are plenty of them around, flying from Ludwigshafen or Saarbrucken fields.'

'Sure are,' Bright Eyes replied easily, his grin still set on his chubby face. 'Radar-equipped Ju-88s.' He shrugged carelessly. 'And can I tell you something else, Major — I ain't even got as much as a peashooter in her to defend myself, if you don't count my personal .38.'

Major Hardt groaned. 'Christ on a crutch! What in Sam Hill have I let myself in for now?'

But there was worse to come. Just as the Field began to black out for the night and Bright Eyes had finished his complicated pre-flight check of the unarmed aircraft, Control came on the air with an urgent message. By the look on Bright Eyes' face, Hardt, squeezed next to him in what had once been the co-pilot seat, could see that it was serious.

Slipping off one earphone, he said quickly. 'There are three Ju-88s circling left to right in a set pattern about a mile from Etain.'

Hardt waited till he had finished with Control and taken off his earphones before asking: 'How are you gonna get airborne, Bright Eyes? I mean once they turn on the runway lights, won't they zoom in and knock you out?'

'That would be the general idea?' Bright Eyes answered nonplussed, fiddling with his switches.

'Then what are you going to do?'

'Well, I could try to get off using my own landing lights. But I guess the Kraut jocks would be able to see my lights from the vantage point they've got up there.'

'So?'

Before Bright Eyes could answer, Control came on the air again. 'What's buzzing cousin?' the pilot snapped into the mike, and listened attentively. An instant later he said. 'No deal. I'm not gonna use any lights. *Period*!'

Obviously whoever was at the other end protested, but Bright Eyes simply grinned in that lazy fashion of his and said, 'Over and out.'

'You're crazy, Captain,' Hardt snapped. 'You'll overshoot and crack up before you're even airborne.'

'Not really,' Bright Eyes answered, in no way offended. 'I'll line up on the end of the strip by compass and make an instrument take-off. I'll keep the compass needle centred and,' he shrugged, 'with a bit of luck, Bright Eyes will make that wild blue yonder once again.'

Hardt gave up, shaking his monstrous bald head, half in admiration, half in dismay. 'Okay, let it go, but don't expect me to recommend you for a medal.' he said.

'Don't need to, Major.' Bright Eyes said, reaching forward to start the Wright Cyclone engines, 'I've got them all already.'

With a roar that shook the plane, the twin engines burst into noisy life. Fortunately both of them had dampers to conceal the exhaust flames and, knowing this, the young pilot taxied the plane slowly down the ramp, across the taxi strip and on to the runway. On the far horizon Hardt could just make out a faint blue, which could well be the exhaust of one of the

Junkers. He had excellent eyesight, but at that moment, he hoped that his eyes were playing tricks on him.

For a moment the young pilot checked his instruments by the blood-red light in his cockpit. Apparently satisfied, he eased the plane round until both his gyro and magnetic compasses were lined up at two-forty degrees. Then he locked the A-20's nose wheel. 'Okay,' he breathed, almost to himself, 'where's the action, Jackson?' Suddenly he pushed the throttles forward. The plane started to roll down the unseen runway. Hardt tensed in the co-pilot's seat. They were on their way!

Hardt knew that on a normal instrument take-off, the pilot could always be helped by his co-pilot looking out of the window and yelling him instructions if the plane veered too close to the grass apron. Even on a very foggy day that was possible. But now Hardt realised that Bright Eyes was entirely on his own; he could not rely on Hardt's unskilled advice from the co-pilot's seat. He would have to get the nine ton ex-bomber off entirely by instrument.

With eyes alert and glued to the flickering, luminous green needles of his two compasses, with deft movements of his gloved hands making the necessary rudder adjustments, he let the A-20 roll slowly down the blacked-out runway. *Two hundred and forty*! He fought the temptation to look out of the cockpit window and kept his eyes on the degree mark by a sheer effort of will, for he knew that once he did so, he would lose his sense of direction.

Next to him Hardt could see the first beads of glistening sweat beginning to form beneath his nostrils and at the edge of his leather flying helmet. The strain must be terrific, he told himself, feeling completely useless for the first time in his adult life.

The A-20 started to gather speed. Faster and faster. Hardt could feel the bump of the tyres as they hit the concrete joints in the runway. Now they were coming closer and closer. He bit his bottom lip hard and prayed fervently that they would soon stop altogether; that would mean they were airborne.

Bright Eyes strained his head forward, staring at the flickering needles till his eyes ached. Time and time again he kicked the rudder to keep the A-20 on course. Would the bastard never get into the air. 'C'mon, baby,' he whispered urgently. 'Feed it to me... *Lift*, willya. *LIFT!*'

Suddenly the A-20 lurched violently. There was the squeal of protesting rubber. The tail swung round. '*Christ on a crutch!*' Hardt began. Bright Eyes reacted immediately. Just before the right wheel went over the edge of the concrete on to the grass, he caught her. Before Hardt could finish his cry of alarm, he had the plane back on course.

Hardt breathed a fervent sigh of relief. An instant later the harsh thump-thump of the runway stopped suddenly. It was replaced by the soft purr of the Wright Cyclone engines.

Bright Eyes turned and grinned at Hardt, his boyish face lathered in a sweat. 'On a wing and a prayer as they say — a cruddy wing and a prayer.'

Hardt nodded weakly. He didn't trust himself to speak.

Fifteen minutes passed. They had circled the beleaguered city of Metz twice. There was no flak and no searchlights, and the blackout was almost perfect. But here and there a couple or so blue lights were sufficient for the keen-eyed pilot to identify known German positions. Now the cabin was very quiet with the pilot flying with one hand, the other tracing their route on his contour map, the contours drawn in mauve for red night-sight reading. Beside him on the seat, his discarded earphones squawked continuously.

'Recognise it?' Bright Eyes asked once, looking up from his map.

'Sounds like Kraut,' Hardt answered.

'Yeah, it's Ludwigshafen fighter control. Always listen to it on these jobbies. Can't understand a word of it, but it's company, isn't it?' He grinned suddenly. 'Sounds like a lot o' ducks fucking, don't it?'

Another five minutes passed. They had been airborne nearly half an hour now. Hardt began to worry. Perhaps the young pilot's ability wasn't what it was cracked up to be at 3rd Army HQ. Surely they should have found the place by now?

It was just about then that Bright Eyes let his map slide to the floor. Very casually, he said, 'I guess we're about there now.'

'Morte d'Homme, you mean?'

'Yeah. Funny kinda name. *Death o' man*! Hope it ain't an omen.'

'Eh?'

'Well, Major, in exactly five seconds flat you and me is going to light a little candle — and that's no fish-eater's altar down there. Okay, here we go.' Next instant he reached forward and flicked a switch.

Hardt recoiled, his handsome face contorted with shock at the fierce white glare which had abruptly turned darkest night into brightest day. Below, the ground was lit up, every single detail of the war-torn landscape immediately visible. His eyes narrowed to slits against the harsh incandescent glare, Hardt caught a swift glimpse of camouflaged concrete hidden by dense firs. 'There to the left,' he ordered. 'Quick!'

'Roger.'

Bright Eyes banked the plane hurriedly, the burning white light swinging with him.

A pentagon shape came into view, perched on the narrow crown of a thickly wooded hill.

'Can you take her in lower?' Hardt asked excitedly, forgetting the obvious danger now.

'Sure,' Bright Eyes said easily, 'nothing's too good for the boys in the service. But not too much. Otherwise one of those Kraut sentries down there is going to goose us with his bayonet.'

He dropped the A-20 a further two hundred feet, his engines throttled back to what was virtually stalling speed. Angry red and white tracer started to come from below, curving towards them in a slow arc which gathered speed with every second. Machine gun bullets began to rattle against their metal sides like heavy summer raindrops on a tin roof. Both Hardt and Bright Eyes ignored them.

'Do you see those steel domes — over there? Have you got them now?'

Bright Eyes craned his neck over the controls. 'Yeah.'

'They'll be the Battery. One ... two ... three ... four, yeah four of them. Yes, thats the Führer Battery all right.' Bright Eyes puffed out his lips. 'They'd be a sonuvabitch to bomb from the air. Nobody could get through the trees at that angle and hit 'em with any certainty. And the Ninth TAC's dive-bombers are too inaccurate for a job of that kind.'

'Yes,' Hardt agreed, 'that's my thinking too. Besides, God knows how deep the guns themselves are beneath those steel domes. Fifty, sixty feet!'

Bright Eyes whistled softly through his front teeth. 'That ain't peanuts, brother,' he said. 'So how ya gonna do it?'

'I'd like to know that myself! Look, let's have one more run over here so I can note the positions —' He never finished his request.

WHAM! *WHAM*! The red burning 20mm shells from the Ju-88s came winging towards them like a swarm of angry hornets. Next instant the two burning lights fell out of the sky above them, converged on the A-20, and the Junkers night bombers shrieked past on each side with a thunderous, ear-splitting scream, clearing the aircraft by feet. For one moment the whole plane seemed to pause in midair, cringing, like a dumb animal being tormented by two great metallic horse flies.

Bright Eyes reacted immediately. He kicked his right rudder, then his left. The A-20 fishtailed alarmingly. 'Makes it more difficult for the bastards to get in a deflection shot,' he gasped, as some four hundred feet away, the fighter bombers' deadly cannon started to chatter again. Violet lights crackled the length of the Junkers' noses. Tracer hissed through the air.

Bright Eyes ripped back the twin throttles. Hardt lurched forward, saved only by his belt. Just as the fighter bombers hurtled towards them like fire streaked darts, Bright Eyes thrust down the nose. The A-20 dropped like a stone. Behind, the lead Junkers, unable to pull out of its dive in time, hit the ground. There was a violent crash. A great ball of flame unrolled and shot upwards. Hardt caught a quick glimpse of metal fragments spiralling up, stark black against the blood-red of the fire. Next instant, Bright Eyes had jerked up the controls and the A-20 was climbing at an impossible angle. 'Crazy Kraut kid,' he gasped through gritted teeth. 'Now he's gone and broke his toy airplane.'

Hardt tried to smile, but found his jaw muscles wouldn't work the way he wanted them to. 'Yeah,' he gasped. 'You might well say that.'

One hand on the controls, which were shaking violently as if about to disintegrate at any moment, Bright Eyes slipped on his earphones and cried, 'Petite Contrôle … Petite Contrôle … do you read me?'

Apparently they did, for he called the next moment, 'Bright Eyes… Bright Eyes.… how many bandits have you got?'

Somewhere down below the ground control radioman, with a powerful radar set at his disposal, fed the young pilot the information he needed and Hardt, tense next to him, could see it wasn't good.

'Well?' he demanded, as Bright Eyes slipped off the earphones.

'Positive, I'm afraid,' Bright Eyes answered, his face very grim. 'Two positive Kraut identifications between us and base.'

'Forget Etain then,' Hardt said hastily, as Bright Eyes levelled out. 'What about trying for Tours?'

Bright Eyes shook his head firmly. 'No deal, Major. I'd never make it. We're running out of juice and I'm not in a mood to try a crash landing this time of night. It's either Etain or nothing.' He forced a grin. 'What do they say in infantry? There are no atheists in foxholes. Okay, so I'm suddenly converted. *Better start praying, Major.*'

The two Junkers caught up with them five miles east of Etain Field, just as they were crossing the US lines. One moment there was nothing but eternal silent blackness, broken only by the steady drone of their engines, the next the air was torn apart by the angry chatter of German cannon.

The perspex of the cockpit shattered into a crazy spider's web. Splinters of plexiglass coated their flying helmets and an icy wind struck them violently.

Bright Eyes reacted at once. He dropped the A-20 to the left as the Junkers homed in again. 20mm shells stitched a deadly pattern the length of their fuselage. Blow after blow! The whole plane trembled with the impact. There was the sudden nauseating stink of gas. Evil blue flames started to lick up from somewhere to the rear of the plane. The tip of their left wing went. It began to burn too.

'Hello, Bright Eyes,' Petite Contrôle's voice crackled faintly from the earphones on the seat. 'You're being attacked.'

'Ya don't say,' Bright Eyes cracked, his face streaming with sweat as he tried to fight the plane's tendency to side-slip.

'Bright Eyes … Bright Eyes,' the controller called. 'If you're hit — *bail out … bail out!*'

'Get on to that stupid jerk,' the pilot yelled. 'Tell him to depress his transmitter key … we'll home on it.'

Hardt grabbed the earphones, just as the Junkers zoomed in again at three hundred mph, cannon chattering, filling the night air with the vicious red tracer.

'Hello Petite Contrôle … hello Petite Contrôle, the Captain says depress your transmitter key.'

'Yean, yeah, I read ya,' an angry Bronx voice interrupted, 'I read ya good. Okay, buddy, it's your goddam neck. *Over!*'

As the needle of the radio compass picked up Control's signal, Bright Eyes eased the crippled A-20 round, flames streaming from its rear. A Junkers roared in. Hardt could see its nose light quite clearly. He tensed. This was it!

But nothing happened. A moment later the twin-engine night fighter veered off to the right, obviously satisfied that the American plane would never make it back to its base. In a few seconds the blue light of its exhausts had disappeared into the darkness. The Germans had broken off their attack, heading for the safety of Ludwigshafen Air Base before the American fighters caught them. They were on their own at last.

In grim silence Bright Eyes fought to get the crippled plane back to base. Tensely he watched the altimeter until the trembling needle hit two hundred feet, then he levelled out, banking east until he was on course for the Moselle somewhere down below in the pitch darkness.

'We'd never be able to jump at this height,' he explained, not taking his eyes from the controls for one instant. 'But at least the Kraut jocks wouldn't dare jump us down here. Now I'm going to keep her at eighty per cent max power. I'm losing gas but —'

The plane's nose dropped alarmingly. Fresh splinters of dislodged plexiglass showered their frozen faces. With all his strength Bright Eyes jerked back the controls. 'Lift you sonuvabitch!' the pilot cried fiercely. '*Up ... up ... up!*'

Desperately he twisted the control wheel all the way to the right. Shattered equipment slithered the length of the dying plane. Viciously he kicked the right rudder to raise the left wing. To no avail! He tried another tack, his face gleaming with glass splinters. He pulled back the right engine throttle and gunned the left engine at maximum power. For an instant the A-20's sideways slipping halted. But only for a moment. Abruptly the damaged burning left wing flipped up from the horizon. Bright Eyes caught her just in time before she did a complete roll to the right. He levelled her out. But again she started to slip to one side.

He shook his head, not daring to take his hands from the controls. 'No dice,' he gasped, as if he had just been running a long race, 'I can't hold the bitch.'

'What now?'

'I'm gonna crash-land.'

'*Down there — in this darkness!*' Hardt exclaimed.

'It's the only way … and we've got the light, remember.'

Not waiting for Hardt's reply, he chopped the throttles. With the same hand he flipped off all the switches. Suddenly there was no sound save the hiss of the wind. They were coming down fast.

'Okay, Major, get on to that light.'

'Roger.'

'Right — *now!*' Bright Eyes snapped tautly.

Hardt flicked the switch.

Down below the flat wet countryside sprang into view in white surprise. Bright Eyes narrowed his gaze. 'The Moselle', he announced, 'over to the right.'

Hardt craned his neck. He could just make out the silver snake of the river perhaps a couple of miles away. 'Do you think we're going to make it?'

'We'd better!' was the pilot's tight-lipped reply, as he fought to keep the plane from stalling altogether.

The river came even closer. Hardt could see its broad expanse between the low cliffs quite clearly. But he could also see the fields looming up to meet them and the tree tops which seemed almost in touching distance. He swallowed hard, his body dripping with sweat in spite of the night cold. They were only about fifty feet above the ground now.

'Come on … come on,' Bright Eyes urged, pushing at the dead controls, almost as if he were forcing the stricken plane physically to its destination. 'Make with the feet, you stupid bitch!'

But the A-20 did not 'make with the feet'. Suddenly she lurched to one side. 'Cover your face!' Bright Eyes yelled in a frenzy of alarm. '*Quick, man!*'

Without waiting to see if Major Hardt was obeying his order, he drew his feet up from the floor and threw his arms, tightly clasped together, elbows forward, against his face.

Not a moment too soon! The A-20 went into a steep dive. It hit the field with a sickening thump and rose high into the air. When it struck the ground again, its right tyre burst like a 75mm shell exploding. Crazily the A-20 shimmied from side to side. The burning left wing banged the ground. It snapped off immediately.

Bright Eyes came out of his foetal position and grabbed the controls. Screaming unintelligible curses, he fought the plane as it careened and skidded between the ancient oaks which bordered the field. By a miracle he managed to get through them. Then his luck ran out at last. The undercarriage collapsed. A fierce rending sounded as the ground tore the plane's guts out. Metal shrieked horrifyingly. They slithered forward at a hundred mph, enveloped in a huge cloud of mud and dust, trailing red-hot shards of metal behind them. There was a tremendous crash and the A-20 came to a final halt, its right wing crumpled like a banana skin against the shattered stone byre which had stopped them at last.

For what seemed a long time nothing moved in the crashed plane. Then, as the GIs of the 90th Infantry, dug in along the Moselle, started to clamber out of their muddy foxholes and run across the wet field shouting hoarsely, Major Hardt stirred.

He shook his numb head and drove away the crazy, whirling world of fire and shrieking. His mouth was full of something wet, hot and slightly salty. Curiously he spat into his hand. His palm was crimson. He wiped it on his trouser leg. Slowly he turned to the pilot. He was slumped over the shattered controls, still strapped in his harness, his head bent over the wheel at a curious angle.

'Hey, are you okay?' he asked thickly through a mouthful of blood.

The young pilot did not move.

With a hand that felt as if it possessed fingers as fat as German sausages, he reached out and grabbed the pilot's collar. 'Come on, Bright Eyes, wake up.'

But Bright Eyes would never wake again and his eyes were no longer bright. They stared sightlessly from a face which looked as if someone had thrown a handful of jelly at it. T-Force's new mission had claimed its first victim...

CHAPTER 4

Major Hardt looked out of the window of his office in Verdun's *Maginot Caserne*, named after that infantry sergeant who had lost his leg on the gaunt heights above and who, as war minister in the Thirties, had created the vaunted Maginot Line. Hardt sniffed at the thought. The Line had protected France against a second Verdun well enough, but had made her so complacent that she'd rolled over like a tame dog when the Krauts had arrived in '40 and allowed them to scratch her fat soft underbelly. It had been a walk-over for the Germans.

Outside it was drizzling again. Thin, cold and bitter. But that was nothing new. It seemed to have been drizzling ever since T-Force had arrived at the grim French fortress city which in 1916 had seen the greatest blood-letting in modern history. The men assembling down below in the cobbled square, their helmets shining and their raincoats slick with the rain, did not even seem to notice; the drizzle had become part of the background at *Maginot Caserne*.

Curiously, Major Hardt stared at T-Force which he had created back in North Africa in 1943 to be Patton's 'eyes and ears': a fast moving reconnaissance outfit a hundred and twenty strong, capable of moving across any type of terrain in their Staghounds and White half-tracks, and reporting directly to the 3rd Army Commander. There weren't many of his veterans left now, after the Bridge at Pontaubault.

Out front was his Executive Officer, 1st Lieutenant Clarence van Fleet, who had been with him from the start. In spite of his nickname 'Clarry' and his well-bred accent, as befitted the son of a Boston millionaire, he was a born killer, fond of maintaining that 'the knife is the most civilised of weapons'. And the statement was not mere words; the deadly knife he always kept stuffed down the side of his combat boot was his favourite weapon.

Next to him 'Big Red', the outfit's top Sergeant, chivvying and bullying the men into some sort of order, was another veteran. His broad face as bright red as his hair, the First Sergeant's preferred way of maintaining discipline was with his ham like fists. Hardt was still waiting for him to present a single member of T-Force to him on a disciplinary charge; and there were plenty of tough babies among the vets who would have worn holes in their CO's mat in a normal outfit.

Triggerman, for example, his own gunner, a hot-tempered Italian-American, who had reputedly fled the States in '39 to join the *le Régiment du Légion Étrangère* with his sidekick 'Dutchie' Schulze because, as a Mafia 'soldier', he had double-crossed his local *capo*. Ever since Hardt had taken him over from the Foreign Legion in '43, Triggerman had been in trouble one way or another. His occasional puffed cheek or black eye, courtesy of Big Red, had been evidence of that; but not one word of it had ever reached Hardt's office.

Groves, an ex-New York hackie and another former Legionnaire, was another potential trouble-maker. As undersized and just as hot-tempered as Triggerman, he was nicknamed 'Wheels', gained from his inevitable reply when asked to march: '*Hike*, didya say, Sarge? *Hell no, gimme wheels brother and let me ride.*'

But the worst of the bunch was the little Cockney Smithers, known naturally among his T-Force buddies as 'Limey'. Where the little Cockney, whose main aim in life was (as he often boasted to his cronies) 'to get as much of the other as I can before it drops off in me hand', had been before he had found him in Algiers, Major Hardt did not know. Nor did he attempt to enquire, then or ever afterwards. All he knew was that Limey, who had once served with the élite British Phantom Reconnaissance in the desert, was an outstanding radio operator who could bounce a message further than any other operator he, Hardt, had ever come across in his eight year Regular Army career.

As he picked up his helmet liner, prior to going down, he took one last glance at the faces of the men who made up his own personal crew. Big Red, his face brick-red with shouting; Limey, his narrow clever face cast in its usual cheeky grin; Dutchie, his good-humoured features as wrinkled and brown as old leather from his years in the Desert; Wheels, his nose and cheeks smudged with oil as always, obviously the result of tinkering with the beloved engine of the team's irreverently named half-track, Old Baldy; and Triggerman, his skinny body loaded down with grenades, combat knives, a .45 and an officer's grease gun, stolen somewhere or other, his dark olive face sullen and threatening. 'Not exactly the Point,' he told himself as he turned to the door, 'but a tough bunch of babies. That's for sure!'

As he stepped into the cobbled courtyard, Big Red called T-Force to attention with a bellow which sent the crows, nesting in the stark trees at the edge of the barracks, into the grey sky cawing in hoarse protest.

Major Hardt acknowledged Big Red's rigid salute. 'Thank you, Red. At ease!'

The top Sergeant swung round smartly like the Regular Army man he was and barked at the top of his tremendous voice, as if the men facing him were four hundred and not a mere four feet away from him, '*At ease, men!*'

From the other side of the courtyard, van Fleet looked at Hardt enquiringly. Hardt nodded and van Fleet sped away to carry out the task the two officers had discussed half an hour before, while the Major began his briefing.

'Men, as you all know, T-Force is General Patton's eyes and ears. Now the General has given us another of his special missions.'

'Not another Lulu like that goddam bridge,' Triggerman snarled. 'Brother was that some Snafu!' The undersized Mafia killer ignored the sudden threatening look on Big Red's crimson face. 'We can use missions like that like a hole in the head, Major.'

'No,' Hardt said firmly, 'there'll be no more snafus. This mission is going to be planned down to the last detail. Don't you worry, you new men,' he flashed a glance along the ranks of the replacements, their young fresh faces keen but a little apprehensive. 'I want no casualties, if it's at all possible, on this one. Red,' he snapped at the Sergeant, 'the map.'

While Big Red hurried to the blanket-shrouded map on a blackboard trestle, which was set up in the centre of the cobbled square, Hardt ordered the men to break ranks and gather round the detailed plan of Metz's defences. It had been prepared specially for him by Colonel Koch's intelligence staff.

'Okay, fellers,' he began, 'this is the big picture.' Swiftly he told them what he had learnt from General Patton two days before and what he had discovered on his ill-fated flight with Bright Eyes, watching their faces carefully for any reaction while he did so. But even among the youngest of them he could detect no trace of fear. With a quickening of his heart, he realised that Patton had been right when he had stated that T-Force had received the cream of the ripple-dipples. 'Right, so you see the basic problem. Any questions before I carry on?' he looked enquiringly along their ranks.

'Yessir.' It was the Cockney.

'Yes, what is it, Limey?'

'Do you think I could get an immediate transfer to the Quartermaster Branch, sir?'

Hardt laughed and his men grinned. He knew Limey. He was cunning, resourceful, nobody's fool — and very tough. A good man to have along on a mission like this. 'I'll think about it, Limey — *after we get back.*'

'*If* we get back,' Limey muttered, but no one heard him in the laughter which greeted Hardt's words.

'So how are we gonna do it?' Hardt answered his own question. 'Well, for a start, the front door to Metz is very decidedly closed to us. With those four forts peering down their throats, the guys of Ninety Div daren't even raise their eyebrows during daylight hours. There are Kraut snipers everywhere.' He let the information sink in for a moment. 'So I've decided we're gonna use the back door.'

'How do you mean, sir?' Dutchie asked in that slow, lumbering manner of his.

'Like this.' He tapped the map. 'Third Army's main effort is concentrated on the Moselle crossings — *here* — below those four forts. They know darn well we're gonna need them before we get across in force and push on into Krautland. As a result, both we and the Krauts have got our best men in the line there. Our recent Operation Thunderbolt, which we loused up pretty badly, must have convinced the Krauts that we're making a big play for those forts. Now, naturally, the rest of the Metz perimeter is defended. But the Krauts have been cut off from the Fatherland for nearly a month now and no further troops can get into Metz to make up for their casualties. So what do they do?' Again he answered his own question. 'Wherever there are good natural or artificial defences, they thin out the line and put in their second grade troops.'

From somewhere in the ancient barracks' former stables, there came the thick choking cough of a tank motor, reluctant to start in the chill morning air. Hardt raised his voice so that everyone could hear him above the noise. 'Now one such spot is Maizières-les-Metz seven miles north of Metz — *here*. It's a mining town, which our guys nearly took in September. But they got bogged down in the place's slag heaps, which provided the Krauts with an ideal artificial defensive line to the northwest — here. For over two weeks last month, the 357th Infantry slogged it out with the Krauts, but in the end they gave up. They were taking too many casualties for General Patton.'

Over in the old stables, the tank motor had finally started and the driver, whoever he was, was gunning the engine, making sure that it wouldn't stall on him again. Big Red flushed angrily at the noise which was disturbing the vital briefing. But at that particular moment there was nothing he could do about it, if he didn't want to miss the CO's instructions. All the same, he promised himself hotly, once the parade was dismissed, he a find the driver of that tank and feed him one of his celebrated 'knuckle sandwiches'. And how!

'Now the situation in Maizières-les-Metz is like this. We hold the northern part of the town with a battalion of black volunteer soldiers. The Krauts have moved out the People's Grenadier Division which held it during the September fighting and have replaced it with an Ear and Eye Battalion.'

'And what the hell is that, Major, when it's at home?' Limey asked, expressing the bewilderment of them all.

Hardt grinned. It was the question he had anticipated. 'Well, for dietary and medical reasons the Krauts have been grouping their 4Fs together in battalions. For instance, all their second-line troops who have some sort of stomach trouble are formed into Stomach Battalions so that it's easier for their hash slingers to feed them the special sort of chow they need. It's that kind of special battalion which is holding Maizières-les-Metz. There is one other thing, fellers. Those men have taken exactly one hundred and fifty casualties in the last seven days alone.'

'How, sir?' Wheels asked.

Hardt's face set severely as he replied. 'S-mines,' he snapped brutally.

'*Jesus H. Christ*!' someone groaned. '*Them murderous bastards.*' He expressed all their feelings: everyone in T-Force, veteran and replacement, knew of the frightening antipersonnel mine, which the engineers could not detect by normal electronic means because it was fitted with a nonmagnetic wooden case.

'Yes,' Hardt continued, 'the Krauts have holed up between the town's railroad station and city hall — here and here. They've covered the approach roads with antitank guns and bazooka teams, and the open spaces between the railroad tracks — here — and the slag heaps, the best place for our infantry to attack, with S-mines. That's where the boys took all their casualties last week.'

Hardt paused for a moment, watching their faces, knowing what they were all thinking at that moment. All of them had heard of the terrible damage the S-mine inflicted on the human body. Indeed you were lucky if the initial explosion only took your foot off. Filled as they were with steel ball bearings, the deadly devices had emasculated many an unwary soldier, peppering his crotch as they shot upwards in their scores. As the front line soldiers of the Third said in awed voices whenever they heard the name 'S-Mine': 'Better off a stiff, than a goddam living tenor with his pecker shot off!'

'All the same,' he continued when he felt they had had enough time to digest the horrifying news, 'Maizières-les-Metz is gonna be our backdoor into the Kraut positions.'

'But Major,' Dutchie objected, 'the S-mines.'

'I know. It's just because of the mines and the Krauts' belief that we won't attack through that area that we're going to use it.' He grinned suddenly. 'You see, Intelligence has come up with something which —'

But he never finished. At that moment there was the roar of a tank motor, as the driver gave it full power to negotiate a corner. An instant later a great lumbering British Churchill tank came edging its way awkwardly round the corner, a smiling van Fleet on its turret, a black British Tank Corps beret perched jauntily at the back of his head. But it was a Churchill, the like of which T-Force's veterans had never seen in their long battle experience before. Attached to the square glacis plate, there was a great round box from which hung what looked like a collection of iron chains, the sort used by Mid-Western farmers to harness their plough-horses.

'Jesus wept,' Triggerman snarled over the rusty rattle and clatter of the thirty ton British tank, 'what the hell's that supposed to be!'

'One of the British funnies,' Hardt bellowed. He cupped his hands around his mouth and yelled at van Fleet. 'Okay, Clarry, don't stand there grinning like a goddam monkey up a stick! Give 'em a demonstration!'

Van Fleet's grin vanished immediately. He bent swiftly and whispered to someone hidden below in the turret.

The tank's engine roared to a crescendo. The long chains trembled. Suddenly the great round box started to revolve, slowly at first, then with increasing speed. Abruptly the chains were flying round, whistling through the air and striking the cobbles, so that blue sparks flew everywhere, eight to ten feet ahead of it.

Slowly smiles of understanding began to dawn on the spectators' faces, as Hardt, delighted that he was already beginning to convince them of the feasibility of his plan, shouted to van Fleet to end the little demonstration. 'Yeah,' he cried, when the tank's motors died down to a low diesel whine, 'meet the British Flail, fellers — the way we're gonna get through that goddam minefield...'

CHAPTER 5

Somewhere up the pot-holed, battle-littered road an 88mm was banging away like a hammer in hell. At regular intervals the hundred pound shells slammed into the American-held part of Maizières. Next to the road, the little stone house which was K Company's HQ shuddered each time, like a destroyer at full speed when it hits a bow-wave; and inevitably, Captain Kee, the Company Commander, crouched over the kitchen table in the white hissing glare of the Coleman lamp, jumped nervously at each fresh explosion.

Hardt looked at van Fleet significantly, but said nothing. The lean Infantry Captain, wearing the gold-rimmed pince-nez of a high school teacher of maths which he had been before he volunteered for the Army, was obviously about at the end of his tether. Privately Hardt gave him about another week before he cracked up completely, like so many other infantry commanders in the Third were doing now, and was sent back to the States as yet another case of combat fatigue.

'Okay,' Kee said wearily, staring blankly at the glaring lamp, 'this is the set-up. The Krauts are dug in on either side of the Thionville-Maizières road, about a hundred yards further on from here. They've got antitank and according to my scouts, about a dozen guys armed with panzerfausts. Now it's my plan to take my men up either side of that road at dusk — say eighteen hundred hours at this time of the year. Your guys can be in position by then, I guess?'

Hardt nodded, wondering what the skinny bespectacled Captain must have gone through in these last two weeks to make him look as he did: a dead shell who seemed simply to be going through the motions, kept going by sheer effort of will.

'Okay. We'll move out then and create the diversion you'll need to cover your approach and the noise that Limey contraption will make.'

'*Diversion*, you call it,' Hardt said as the 88mm cracked again and its shell came howling down the road like a hound out of hell. 'That looks a pretty tough position for your boys —'

'Not boys, *men*, Kee interrupted, not taking his eyes off the hypnotic glare of the lamp. 'Every man-jack of them volunteered from a nice safe job behind the line to come into the infantry. Fifty per cent of them gave up rank in order to get the chance to fight, Major. They're not boys, not black trash, shades or any other damn name of prejudice we've been finding for them over these last centuries — they're simply black fighting men —'

'Captain, we sympathise — we honestly do. It was simply a slip of the tongue,' van Fleet's soft yet somewhat sinister voice cut in politely. 'But I wonder if we could get back to our *moutons*, please.'

For the first time since they had entered his tumble-down HQ, the worn-out Captain took his eyes off the lamp, 'Okay, I'm sorry, but if you knew what kind of crap this battalion has had to take from those damned prejudiced southern rednecks' who — Oh, well, let's forget it.' He pinched the bridge of his nose, as if he were very tired. 'I guess my fellers will be able to keep it up for about thirty minutes before they run out of steam. They're keen, but they've taken a terrific beating and I'm down to half my riflemen.'

Hardt nodded his understanding. He had taken, a quick look at the enemy positions before they had slipped into the blacked-out HQ. The German-held stone miners' cottages, their metre thick walls pocked with bullets now, were like miniature fortresses. 'Thirty minutes will be enough, Captain. And may I say, I appreciate the efforts of you and your *men*.'

For a moment Captain Kee did not reply. Instead he tried to light a *Lucky Strike*. But the hand which held the match trembled so badly that he had to hold it with the other before he managed to do so. Then he said bitterly, 'Sure, everybody will appreciate us — when we're all safely dead...'

'Kay, I'll take the point myself,' Kee whispered to the men crouched behind the cover of the house. 'Benny and Washington, you cover me.'

'Sir,' the two sergeants replied in soft unison.

'The rest of you follow at five yard intervals.' Kee hesitated. He couldn't see their faces in the darkness, just sensed them there. Ex-cooks and carpenters, redcaps and bellhops, who had been third-class citizens all their lives and who were now thousands of miles away from their homes fighting for democracy. 'Kee's Boys', they called them in the rest of the Division, yet the Captain felt a warm glow of pride in his reviled third-class citizens at that moment. They wouldn't let him down, he knew that. 'And listen,' he continued, 'I don't want any of you fellers taking any unnecessary risks. We hit them, keep them pinned down for thirty minutes and then we get out again — *no more*. Got it guys, eh?'

'Yes Captain, sir,' the whispered replies came in the thick accents of the South.

'Kay, let's go.'

Crouched low, Kee and the two buck sergeants hissed down the street, sticking to the shadows cast by the shattered houses like grey ghosts. They came to the first line of German wire. While Kee and Benny covered him, Washington slung his MI and ran his hands along the barbs. Behind them the rest of the company had come to a halt, weapons at the ready.

'Booby trapped?' Kee asked anxiously.

'Nope.' Washington grunted, 'but I think ... they've got a can of rocks... *Yep!*' He tugged and the can full of pebbles, which would have warned any German sentries out there in the darkness if they had blundered into it, came free. He lowered it gently to the cobbles.

Wordlessly, as if it were a long-established routine, Kee dropped on his back at the base of the wire and reached up the big wire-cutters. Washington followed suit and while Benny covered the two of them they took the strain.

The first strand parted. Its snap sounded like an MI going off. Above them Benny tensed, grease gun at the alert. But nothing happened. There was no sound save for the steady, persistent rumble of the barrage in the distance, the ever present background music of war. Swiftly they cut the remaining strands.

Kee rose to his feet and picked up his carbine. His heart was thumping like a trip-hammer and ne could hardly control the trembling of his hands, although he had drunk nearly a pint of his precious ration Bourbon before they had left. 'Kay,' he forced himself to say, taking the lead again, 'let's get on the ball, guys, *Move it!*'

They 'moved it'.

A minute passed. And another. Now the rest of the company was through the first line of wire, creeping stealthily down each side of the dark street. Far to the east rockets were hissing into the night sky, trailing a shower of brilliant red sparks behind them. But despite his nervousness, Kee knew they had nothing to do with him. Somewhere else along the line, the 90th or 83rd would be putting in a fighting patrol and the Krauts were summoning help, which they usually did by means of signal rockets. He breathed out, a little more at ease. The rockets could well mean the Krauts were concentrating on their line to the east; K Company might take them by surprise after all.

But that wasn't to be.

Suddenly Washington stumbled. Even his eyes had let him down in the pitch darkness. '*Goddam mother-f* —' he began, trying to steady himself. Somewhere along the trip wire he had tumbled across, there was a faint metallic zip, followed by a louder hiss. Even before the device exploded, Kee knew instinctively what it was. '*TRIP FLARE!*' he yelled.

Next instant it rushed into the air, twenty feet high. A crack. A shower of red flame. In a flash the men running along the shadows were bathed in an unreal crimson glare, and the thin-barrelled Kraut spandaus began their deadly work. *Kee's Boys had walked into a trap…*

Half a mile away, T-Force — two half-tracks, two Staghounds and six jeeps — was drawn up under the cover of some battered oaks which lined the track they would take through the minefield. They were effectively concealed from whatever enemy might be in front of them by a huge slag heap. All the same, the veterans, smoking and chatting in the chilly open vehicles, kept their hands cupped carefully around the glowing tips of their cigarettes and pitched their voices low.

In Old Baldy — the name always irritated Hardt although Limey, who had christened the command half-track thus, insisted that it was the name of 'one of yer Yankee mountains, aint it?' — the Commander of T-Force listened idly to the chatter of his crew and wondered yet again at their apparent calm.

'So ya see, fellers,' Dutchie was explaining, 'I was strolling down the street outside Maginot when I sees this gal under the street lamp. She looked kinda of sad to me —'

'Yer, she would do — *to you*,' Limey interrupted.

But Dutchie, the good Catholic, who said his rosary every night, ignored the interruption as unworthy. 'So, I offered her some gum. But she was too proud for that, I could see that. I asked her if she wanted a cigarette. But she seemed to have plenty. Perhaps somebody gave her them as a present —'

'Yeah, I bet they did,' Triggerman sneered, inevitably aggressive as if he were permanently spoiling for a fight, Hardt couldn't help thinking. 'She probably gave you a present too, you dumb ox.'

Dutchie let himself be stopped. He looked at Triggerman's glowing olive face curiously. 'What kinda present do ya mean, Triggerman?'

'Jesus H, can anybody be that dumb!' Triggerman exclaimed to the rest of Dutchie's grinning listeners. 'A nice juicy case of siff, you stupid jerk!'

'Say that again, Triggerman,' Dutchie retorted threateningly, 'and I'm gonna give you a fistful of knuckles, buddy or no buddy o' mine!'

'Aw, go and crap in ya cap —'

Triggerman never finished his contemptuous reply. At that moment the front to their left came to life with frightening suddenness. Signal rockets, green, red and blue, hissed into the night sky, machineguns started to chatter frantically and there was the frenetic snap and crackle of a fire fight.

Hardt sprang into action at once. 'It's Kee, Clarry,' he snapped to his Executive Officer. 'He's run into trouble already… Okay, Red, shoot the works!'

Big Red cupped his huge paws around his mouth. 'All right, youse guys,' he bellowed, knowing there was no need for silence now, '*roll 'em*!'

Just in front of Old Baldy, the special Churchill burst into life. A thick cloud of blue smoke burst from its exhaust. It seemed to act as a signal for the rest. Motor after motor came alive. Nervous young replacements urinated for the last time and sprang into their vehicles. In the jeeps the drivers stamped on the sandbagged floors — extra protection against mines. Behind them in the two Staghounds, the leather-helmeted gunners jerked back the bolts of their .5 machine guns, ready for action.

Hardt waved his right hand around his head. Three times — the signal to move off.

The British Tank Corps Sergeant who commanded the Churchill spotted the glow of Hardt's luminous wristwatch in the darkness. There was a clatter of tracks. Mud splattered up. Rattling, as if it might fall apart at any moment, the metal monster started to move forward. 'Give 'em hell, lads,' Limey shouted after it, 'for the sake of the old regiment and all that!'

'Knock it off!' Big Red commanded thickly.

'Okay, Wheels,' Hardt ordered, taking one quick last look at his crew to check that every man was in position. They were. 'Move out after the Flail!'

'Wilco!' Wheels rammed home first gear, crouched over the wheel as if he were fighting the five-thirty rush hour on Fifth Avenue. The White half-track began to clank after the tank. A minute later they passed the wooden notice board with its crudely painted skull and crossbones and its grim warning in German, '*Achtung-Minen*!'

They had entered the minefield. Now everything depended on Kee's Boys out somewhere to their right and the clumsy monster waddling along the track in front.

Kee saw the Kraut in the same instant as the latter spotted him. But the ex-high school teacher reacted first. He lobbed the fragmentation grenade and ducked. Not a moment too soon. The grenade exploded in a flash of angry red. Razor-sharp splinters of hot steel hissed through the darkness at waist height. The Kraut went down screaming, his body almost sawn in half.

But there were more of them now, running and stumbling out of the first house, firing wildly from the hip as they came. Behind Kee Benny opened up with his carbine, bent on one knee, while Washington sprayed the street with his grease gun. The night was full of confused shouting, curses and the screams of men in agony. '*Sanitäter … Sanitäter!*' the frightened agonised pleas for aid went up on all sides. In vain. None was forthcoming. The Americans were already stumbling and stamping over the writhing bodies.

An elderly German armed with a bayonet tried to rush the point. Washington felled him with a burst to the stomach.

'*A-aah!*' the man screamed and went down, clutching his suddenly bulging guts.

'Guess that cured the bastard's stomach ache for good, Captn!' Washington chuckled, then fell himself with a slug in his head.

Kee groaned and dragged Washington to the nearest wall. But it was no use. Washington was already dead. Standing above the two of them, Benny pumped shot after shot into the shattered window of the next house, as if he were back on the range at Fort Bliss.

'Okay, fellers!' Kee forced himself to shout. 'Come on, let's get the square-headed bastards!'

With a hoarse cheer 'Kee's Boys' swarmed forward, firing as they went. Benny's carbine clattered to the cobbles, knocked from his hands by a burst of mg fire. He didn't even stop. With one and the same movement, he pulled out his gleaming cut-throat razor and slashed it across the face of the German who had fired the burst. He went down screaming like a hysterical woman, hands grabbing frantically for his ruined face. 'Now shake your head, white boy,' Benny grunted and sprang over the writhing body.

Kee was hit in the shoulder. The impact at that close range slammed him against the wall, as if he had been punched by a gigantic fist. His pince-nez clattered to the ground. 'You a'right Captn?' Dimly he could make out Benny's concerned black face, his yellow sick eyes glowing with excitement. 'Yeah,' he gasped. 'It's just a nick … What time is it?'

Benny's arm shot up to reveal his three looted German watches. 'Kraut time says twenty after six, Captn.'

'Thanks, Benny.' He winched with acute pain. 'Okay, come on, let's get the bastards. We'll give Major Hardt another ten minutes —'

His words were cut short by a soft, obscene belch. Next instant the first mortar bomb landed fifty feet behind the company with a harsh, frightening crunch. A straggler was thrown up into the air, a mass of wildly flailing limbs, silhouetted starkly against the blood-red flame of the explosion.

'*Shit, Captn!*' Benny cursed, as the rest of the salvo followed, sending fist-sized fragments of glowing steel hissing through the ranks of the men who were dropping to the cobbles, 'the Kraut bastards have gone and cut us off…'

The first mortar shell landed on Kee's Company in the same moment that the Churchill started its operation. Hardt breathed a sigh of relief; the racket the mortar kicked up would cover the rattle of the flail.

Slowly the giant chains began to gather speed. Hardt could not see them in the darkness, but he could hear their clatter well enough. Spread out in a tight line behind the Churchill, the column started to pick up speed.

For what seemed a long time, nothing happened. To their right, the ugly groan of the German mortars intensified. The whole sky was streaked with multi-coloured tracer. Kee's men were obviously engaged in a hell of a fire-fight, Hardt told himself grimly. But he had no time to concern himself with their fate now. His own position was not exactly rosy either. If the Krauts caught T-Force in the middle of the minefield, they would be in serious trouble — very serious trouble indeed!

The flail struck the first mine. Suddenly there was a thick explosion before them. Violet flame shot into the air. Automatically the crew of Old Baldy opened their mouths to prevent their eardrums from being burst, as the blast hit them in the face. Ball bearings pattered against the White's metal sides and the four ton half-track shuddered violently. But the Churchill flailed onwards completely, unmoved, as if it had just rattled over some kid's balloon.

'Jesus, Major,' Big Red breathed in admiration as Wheels carefully skirted the smoking hole which had appeared so suddenly and frighteningly in the middle of the track. 'That limey tank is a pretty handy toy to have along, ain't it?'

'You ain't shittin', Sarge!' Triggerman agreed, impressed for once.

Limey beamed, his teeth gleaming whitely in the darkness. 'Yer, you Yanks have got a lot to learn from us English chaps yet,' he chortled.

Now the Churchill was deep into the minefield. With chains whirling round at full speed and slapping the earth six to eight feet in front of it in rapid succession, it exploded S-mine after S-mine. Fifty feet behind it, Wheels, sweating heavily in spite of the chill night air, swung the half-track from side to side to avoid the smoking holes, while the rest of the column fought desperately to follow suit.

Hardt glanced anxiously at his wristwatch. He still had five minutes before Kee would start to withdraw. Yet the volume of fire coming from K Company's direction was as heavy as ever. There was no indication as yet that the bespectacled ex-teacher was preparing to break off the action and move back. He heaved a sigh of relief and told himself that despite his acute nervousness, Captain Kee was turning up trumps.

Another hundred yards and another. Soon they knew they would be through. Up ahead the men in the lead half-track imagined they could already see the silhouette of the pithead winding wheels which would indicate that they were approaching Maizières' northern suburbs, where they hoped to find a hiding place in the abandoned workings behind the enemy lines.

From the K Company's direction, the volume of German mortar fire intensified, while the rattle of American small arms fire weakened. Hardt flung another glance at his watch. Kee should have started withdrawing now. What the hell was the matter with him? Had he lost his nerve completely after all and done something damn foolish?

Clarence van Fleet read the look in his CO's face. 'Could be they've gotten themselves pinned down, skipper,' he suggested.

'Could be — the poor bastards!'

And then it happened.

Ahead of Old Baldy, the night was split by a huge hammer of flame. The Churchill was lifted a clear five feet into the air and crashed down again in a great cloud of dust. The half-track trembled violently like a live thing.

'Christ Almighty!' Wheels cried as he braked hard. 'She's run over a mine!'

As Hardt and van Fleet dropped over the side of the White, they knew instinctively what had happened. The Krauts had spread a few antitank mines — perhaps Teller mines — among the rest, a cunning little way of anticipating just this particular eventuality.

Hastily they doubled across to the smoking, immobile Churchill, its left track flopped out in front of it like a severed limb. 'Are you guys all right?' van Fleet called.

'Thank you — yes.' A bereted head appeared at the turret. 'The buggers — the cunning Jerry buggers,' the tank commander cursed a little weakly. 'It was a bloody Teller mine.'

'Yes, that we guessed,' Hardt snapped. 'Okay, what now?' he added anxiously, as the volume of fire from K Company's direction finally began to die away. 'Can you go on?'

Even before the somewhat dazed Sergeant replied, he knew that his answer would be in the negative.

'Okay, we'll just have to chance it on our own,' he decided, knowing that time was running out rapidly now. 'But what about you guys?'

'Don't worry about us, sir,' the Sergeant answered, pulling himself out of the turret and dropping to the ground. 'The way behind us is all right. Me and the lads'll get back okay. It's you lot —' He didn't finish, but Hardt knew well what he meant.

Hardt slapped him lightly on the shoulder. 'Thanks again — anyway. All right, get your Joes out and on the road back. We'll manage now without you.'

'Best of luck, sir,' the Britisher called. A moment later, he and his shaken crew had disappeared hurriedly into the darkness. T-Force was on its own.

Van Fleet looked at Hardt. 'What's the drill now, skipper?' he asked softly.

Hardt shrugged. 'Well, I'm not going to risk any of the men's lives trying to check out the track for S-mines, Clarry. That's for sure.' He paused momentarily. 'Besides we just haven't got the time. Listen to that, will you.' From the direction of K Company's positions there was hardly a sound now, save for the regular harsh crack of what appeared to be pistols.

'What do you make of it, skipper?'

'I hardly dare think, Clarry,' Hardt replied hastily. 'Come on, let's get mounted up and on our way before the Krauts catch us here with our skivvies down.'

'And the Teller mines?'

'We'll worry about that one when we meet it,' was Hardt's sole reply, as Wheels crashed home first gear and the clumsy half-track started to lumber forward again.

They were shooting the survivors now, systematically, disposing of the wounded men as those of the Stomach Battalion who had been farmers in civilian life might have got rid of a lame horse or a sick pig, bending down with a grunt, placing the pistol carefully behind the prisoner's left ear and blasting his skull into a hundred gory fragments.

Kee, his leg shot away, blood spurting from the great wound like from a holed waterpipe, watched them in short-sighted horror, unable to cry out but his chest heaving crazily as if he were sobbing his heart out.

One after another they were massacred with detached, almost clinical, precision in the bloody gutter at the side of the Thionville road. Then it was his turn. A fat, round, middle-aged face swam into view. He caught a whiff of bad breath, coming from a stomach ruined by two months of starving at Stalingrad. He thought he glimpsed tears in the Kraut's eyes, but perhaps he might have been mistaken. Something cold and hard bored against the back of his skull.

'*Jetzt!*' a thick voice breathed. A sharp click. A muffled roar and suddenly his head shattered like a soft boiled egg being struck too hard by a spoon. He screamed once. Then he was dead.

'*Der Letzte,*' the soldier who had shot him called, wiping away his tears with a right hand that was covered to the wrist with blood.

'*Gut,*' the Sergeant snapped. '*Alle zurück zu den Stellungen. Los!*'

They needed no further urging. Their stomach ulcers rumbling menacingly, a warning of what was yet to come after the excitement of the massacre, they began to double back to the safety of the stone houses.

Behind them in the darkness 'Kee's Boys' started to stiffen rapidly in the cold night air.

Now there was no sound save the throaty grumble of motors grinding along in first gear. Twice the half-track in the lead had gone over an S-mine and Old Baldy's crew had ducked instinctively as the ball bearings scythed through the air, pattering against the White's armoured sides like heavy tropical rain. But surprisingly enough their luck held until they had almost reached the crossroads where the track merged with the pavé road that led up to the abandoned mine shafts. Just as Hardt was congratulating himself on getting through safely, there was a sudden, terrifying roar at the end of the column. He swung round just in time to catch a glimpse of the last Staghound's front wheels rearing high in the air as the Teller mine went off below its front axle. It crashed down again, smoke pouring from its shattered motor.

'Hit the brakes, Wheels!' Hardt ordered urgently.

The little ex-cabbie reacted at once. The White skidded to a stop. Instantly the crew bailed out over the side and formed a defensive perimeter, while Hardt and van Fleet, carbines at the alert, doubled back to the stricken Staghound.

The Commander staggered to the ground, bleeding from a deep cut in his head. 'You okay?' Hardt rapped.

'Sure, sure, I'll be all right, Major,' the Corporal said weakly. 'But the driver —'

Hardt pushed past him and clambered into the smoke-filled turret.

The gunner was dead. Sitting bolt upright in the smoky green-glowing interior, a stanchion had penetrated his heart, spearing him neatly to his seat. But below him the driver still moved.

'Clarry, come on — give me a hand,' Hardt ordered urgently.

Together they bent and grabbed the driver under the arms.

'No,' he whispered weakly, when he felt their grip. 'Leave me be, willya.'

'Don't worry, soldier,' Hardt reassured him swiftly, 'We'll soon have you out.' He turned to van Fleet. 'Okay, together now — heave!'

The driver screamed shrilly and came out so easily that they nearly fell over backwards. Then they saw why. *The driver's legs had been severed at the thigh*! If the situation had not been so deadly serious, there would have been something absurdly comic about the way the two legs still remained fixed to the controls, the blood dripping to the torn metal floor. But there was nothing comic about the driver dying on the cold, wet ground next to the shattered Staghound.

Hardt left him to the others and bit his lip. Now he was worried. They were virtually through the minefield, but what would the Germans make of this enemy vehicle so far behind their lines once the dawn revealed its presence, which it surely would? Wouldn't they institute a search throughout the area? Something that would be fatal to their mission. What was he going to do?

Finally he found a way out. Old Baldy edged its way back past the stationary column with Wheels, showing all his skill as a driver, manoeuvring the half-track from side to side on the narrow confines of the track and forcing the wrecked Staghound into the far drainage ditch. Swiftly the whole of the T-Force went to work covering its outline with waste from the nearest slag heap: a human chain working in complete silence in the darkness, racing against time, hearts beating furiously, tensed for that angry challenge which might come at any moment.

In the end it was done, the Staghound covered, however crudely, and the two dead men as well. Hardt said a silent prayer in the hope that they'd concealed the armoured car well enough to fool a casual German observer; then absolutely worn out with the events of the night, he clambered into Old Baldy and ordered: 'Kay, Red, roll 'em, let's get the hell outa here.'

He slumped down wearily next to Wheels, as the column started to move forward into unknown territory. Almost as if he were expressing Hardt's own thoughts, Limey, crouched over his long-range radio, grunted, 'All aboard the *Skylark*. This way for the ruddy mystery tour.' But the usual note of cheerfulness was missing from his raucous voice.

One by one the vehicles disappeared into the night. Now there was no turning back...

PART TWO: METZ

'I'm sick of the siege, of Metz, you Fritzes, the *Amis*, the whole shitty war — and I want out!'

Wanda Lejeune to Kommissar Harzer, Geheime Staatspolizei.

CHAPTER 1

The fat little elderly civilian stood out among the lithe keen young officers of the Field Gendarmerie in their smart uniforms. With his ankle-length leather coat, shabby felt hat, cheap cigar, he could be nothing else but Gestapo. He wore the clothes like a uniform.

'Well?' the senior military policeman snapped finally, putting down his binoculars through which he had been studying the Churchill, wrecked in the middle of the minefield, 'what do you make of it, Harzig?'

In his thirty years in the police, Harzig had learned never to make snap decisions; you survived longer that way. As he had been wont to say to his Secret Police cronies back in Cologne before he had been unlucky enough to be posted to Metz: 'I served under the Kaiser. Later I served under Hindenburg and now I'm serving Adolf. If the Amis ever get this far, I'll probably serve under the Jewish, Roosevelt, too.' And here he would tap his long, pock-marked nose and wink solemnly. 'You see, lads, it's all a matter of knowing when to open your mouth and when to keep it shut.'

Now, carefully, almost daintily, he flicked the ash off his cheap cigar on to the blank, unseeing face of the dead man lying in the gutter at his feet. 'Well, it all depends, Major.'

'Depends on what, man?' the Police Major snapped irritably. The previous July he had received the German Cross in Gold from the Führer personally, for having carried out the execution of four generals involved in the plot to assassinate Hitler; he wasn't afraid of any elderly, time-serving Gestapo man.

'Whether that funny looking contraption out there was by itself or whether it was accompanied — and if it were accompanied, then by whom or what?'

The Major flushed with irritation at this slow, fat man, whom *Generalleutnant der Waffen SS* Priess, the battle commandant of Metz, had attached to his team investigating the mysterious and futile attack on the Stomach Battalion the night before. 'Man,' he barked, 'you're talking in riddles and we haven't got all day. What I want to know — so I can report accordingly to *Generalleutnant* Priess — is why those shitty soldiers attacked last night against a position they couldn't possibly take in a month of Sundays. And what, in three devils' names is a Tommy tank doing here at Metz with the nearest Tommy unit a good hundred kilometres away from here? That's what I want to know, *Herr Harzig.*' He ended with a snort, sensing his junior officers' looks of admiration, knowing that they were telling themselves that the 'Old Man' really knew how to handle the little shit of a Gestapo man.

The placid look on Harzig's fat contented face did not change. He told himself he had been insulted by better men than the hard-faced Police Major and in the end he had seen them all crawling to him in the Gestapo cellars, their pride gone with the teeth he had punched out of their mouths so lovingly, their faces cringing in fear, their breeches stained with their own urine. 'Perhaps you are right, Major, that was a little bit of a riddle. But you see, unfortunately those men who attacked last night suffered a bad accident after they were captured by our brave lads of the Stomach Battalion — shot while trying to escape,' he kicked the dead soldier in the ribs idly, 'that was it, wasn't it, Major?'

The Police Major flushed, but said nothing.

'So we can't ask *them*!'

'*And?*'

'Well, the only other place where we can find out what happened is over there,' he gestured to the east, cigar clenched in his pudgy, beringed fist.

'Heaven, arse and twine, man,' the Major exploded, 'that's a minefield! When it was laid, there was no time to map it out. Nobody but a damned fool would try to get in there.'

Harzig smiled slowly, knowing that the time had come to score off the Police Major, 'With your permission, *Herr Major*, I can…'

Harzig looked at the sullen, hangdog faces of the French prisoners in the back of the truck and winked at the big Headhunter who had them covered with his machine pistol, 'Arseholes up — three cheers for France!' he cried.

The Field Gendarme laughed unnecessarily loud. 'Yer, *Herr Kommissar*' he chortled, 'that was good. Three cheers for *la belle France*! Ho, ho!'

The *Maquis* prisoners, every one of them under sentence of death, did not react. Instead they looked at their scuffed, worn shoes in silence.

'Proper little rays of sunshine, aren't they, Corporal,' Harzig commented. Then the smile vanished from his fat face and he got down to business. 'Now listen to me, you Frogs,' he said in careful French. 'All of you have been sentenced to lose your turnip in due course.' He brought his hand down on the open palm of his other hand as if it were the blade of the axe used by the German executioner in such cases. One of the prisoners — a young man with dark curly hair and a black eye — shuddered visibly, as if he could already visualise that final scene only too well. 'Now I'm giving you a chance to avoid that fate. Do you understand that? If you're good boys and do as you're told, we won't take yer turnips off.'

A faint glow of hope began to burn in their lack-lustre eyes.

'But there is a price to be paid,' he wagged his cigar at them admonishingly. 'There always is, isn't there, Frogs? All right, this is the situation. You see that Tommy tank up the track. I want to examine it. But there's a problem — there are mines.' Harzig did not give them time to consider the frightening possibility. 'Now if you can get me safely through them to that tank, you'll be back in Metz Prison in no time with nothing else to worry about, except where your next bowl of soup is coming from.' He beamed at them suddenly. 'Now isn't that a fair offer, Frogs?'

For a moment there was no sound but an *Ami* Long Tom in the distance, blasting away — purposelessly — at one of the western forts. Then the oldest of the French prisoners, a balding man in the black leather jacket of a workman, spoke, 'Is that a promise, Boche?'

Harzig overlooked the 'Boche'. 'You have it,' he said quickly, 'on my honour as an officer of the *Geheime Staats-polizei*. Now is that good enough?'

The balding Frenchman spat drily in the mud and said something quickly in the local *patois* to the others. The boy with the dark curly hair opened his mouth to object, but the older man waved him to be silent. '*Allez*,' he snapped, and dropped from the truck. 'We'll do it, Boche.'

Gingerly the Frenchman put a foot down on the track. Harzig, standing safely four metres behind him, could see the sweat start up on his face. The Frenchman brought down his full weight. Nothing happened. Standing there, poised on two feet like a child playing hop-scotch, he turned carefully and said something to the others. In a line they began to move forward slowly — infinitely slowly — as if they were walking across a pile of eggs.

Behind them, Harzig nodded to the big, red-faced Headhunter, his machine pistol at the ready. Slowly they, too, began to follow. The minutes passed leadenly, as they progressed at a snail's pace towards the knocked out Tommy tank. Sweating like swine in spite of the October cold, hardly daring to breathe, their faces lathered in sweat, each step made only after an eternity of deliberation, their hearts beating like triphammers, they moved forward.

The Churchill loomed ever larger. Harzig could see the shattered track and the scorched, blackened bogies under which the mine had exploded. Despite his own lack of danger, the Gestapo man could vividly imagine what it must have been like when that mine had gone off; and if a mine could cause that kind of damage to a metal monster like that, what effect would it have on naked, defenceless human flesh! Harzig licked suddenly parched lips and wished he had not been so damned smart with that fool of a Police Major.

Now they were a mere thirty metres away from the wreck. The Maquis prisoners were moving a little quicker now, no longer so tense, as if they already knew they were through the hidden danger. *Twenty metres … fifteen … ten…* Already Harzig's keen eyes were beginning to scan the rough ground around the Churchill for evidence of the presence of other vehicles. *Five metres to go!*

And then it happened. There was a sudden dry crack. Like a twig snapping underfoot in a wood in high summer. For what seemed a long time nothing stirred. The young Frenchman with the curly hair stared down at his feet, as if he couldn't believe that this terrible thing was happening to him. *To him!*

He opened his mouth to scream. Too late, the S-mine exploded with an asthmatic thud. Flame stabbed the grey morning. The Frenchman's face contorted in absolutely unbearable pain. As the cruel metal balls shot straight between his open legs, he grabbed at nothing, his hands transformed into claws trying to climb the rungs of some invisible ladder. Then he was writhing on the ground in his mortal agony, hands clutched fervently to his shattered sex. A minute later he was dead, his knees drawn right up beneath his chin in the position of an unborn baby. And the others were through, their faces the colour of clay, their limbs trembling with uncontrollable violence.

Harzig noted the many tracks almost at once and the way they had skirted the shattered Churchill, heading towards Metz. With his pistol drawn, and urging the leather-coated Frenchman in front of him — just in case — he explored the area around the tank carefully. It didn't take him long to spot the fact that the slag heap had been disturbed. 'Corporal, get those Frogs over here,' he bellowed excitedly, '*at the double*! I've got something here!'

Five minutes later, the sweating, frightened *Maquis* men had uncovered the front of the Staghound and discovered a legless body clad in a blood-stained uniform. Waving them back, almost forgetting the danger in his excitement, Harzig whistled through his gold teeth. 'An *Ami* armoured car — and a dead *Ami* with it.'

'But great crap on the Christmas Tree, *Herr Kommissar*,' the Headhunter exclaimed, lowering his machine pistol. 'What the hell did the *Amis* go to all that trouble to bury their stiff for?'

'What do you mean?'

The Headhunter shrugged carelessly. 'We all know the *Amis* are *meschugge, Herr Kommissar*. But even the *Amis* are not that crazy! You don't go round burying your stiffs in the middle of a battle, do you?'

'*Naturlich*, unless you —' Harzig caught himself in time. In police work, he had found out, you never told anybody, even your colleagues, more than was absolutely necessary. All too often the bastards would claim the credit for your discoveries themselves.

'Unless what, Herr Kommissar?' the Headhunter persisted.

'Nothing,' Harzig snapped. 'All right, let's get on our hindlegs and out of this dump.'

'*Jawohl, Herr Kommissar*', the Headhunter bellowed at the top of his voice, as if he were back on the parade ground. 'And the Frogs?'

His mind full of what he had just discovered, Harzig did not even bother to reply. As if it were a matter of no importance, he crooked his right forefinger and jerked it back swiftly a couple of times.

'*Verstanden, Herr Kommissar,*' the Headhunter said almost joyfully. He swung his massive bulk round and faced the prisoners. '*Allez, allez, vite,*' he commanded self-importantly, 'everybody over here.'

'*Sale Con!*' they grumbled. But they formed a line in front of the grinning military policeman obediently enough.

He waited till they were all in position and then, with great deliberation, he clicked off the Schmeisser's safety catch. The Frenchmen started, their faces suddenly very pale. 'What is this, Boche?' the elder of them asked. 'You promised —'

'Hold yer water!' the Headhunter interrupted him brutally. He raised the vicious-looking machine-pistol and pointed its muzzle directly at them, enjoying the look of fear on their faces, as they realised what he was going to do. One of them raised his hands, as if he thought the naked flesh might protect him from the cruel steel; another started to sob suddenly. 'But Boche, we did what you asked,' the elder began.

In that same instant, the Headhunter pressed the trigger of his Schmeisser. It chattered into life. The prisoners were galvanised into crazy, violent action, flailing their arms, their tortured limbs jerking as if at the command of a puppet master suddenly gone mad.

Harzig, standing twenty metres away, staring at the wrecked tank, did not even seem to hear. His mind was full of two overwhelming questions: *where had the Amis gone — and for what purpose?*

CHAPTER 2

'*Heil Hitler!*'

Generalleutnent der Waffen SS Hermann Priess, Metz's Battle Commandant, looked up sharply from his papers. In a flash he had taken in Harzig's shabby, leather-coated figure, summed him up and filed him away in the filing cabinet which he called a brain. '*Heil Hitler!*' he rapped. But there was none of the weary casualness of Harzig's greeting in his use of the phrase. The two words were uttered with the harsh fervour of the fanatical National Socialist he was. 'I'll give you five minutes, Harzig,' he said, putting down his pen and lining it up unconsciously with the papers lying on his desk. 'We're expecting a new *Ami* attack — I'm a busy man. Now then what happened at Maizières last night?'

Harzig shuffled his feet noisily. But when no offer to sit down came, he shrugged so that his leather coat creaked and began his account of what he had seen in the minefield outside Maizières-les-Metz.

Priess listened in attentive silence until the elderly Gestapo man had finished. 'You mean that you think the *Amis* used the device to break through our lines and are presently somewhere *within* the garrison?' he barked finally, his bold dark eyes flashing angrily.

Harzig nodded.

'But to what purpose, Harzig?'

The Gestapo man smiled carefully. 'That is perhaps expecting too much of me, *Herr General.* I am just a simple policeman, not a military officer like yourself. But I presume there must be plenty of targets or possibilities. Perhaps they are simply a reconnaissance force, like the one the *Amis* ran into Fortress Aachen last month when they penetrated our lines in German uniform. Perhaps they are here to sabotage one of our installations. Perhaps they are a murder squad, out to kill someone like yourself,' He shrugged, and again his scuffed coat creaked like a pair of old bellows. 'I don't know — I'll leave that problem to the Field-Greys.'

General Priess did not need to be told what the Gestapo man thought of the Field-Greys — the *Wehrmacht;* the look of his round, red face sufficed. But he ignored the look and demanded, 'And what is being done by the *Feldgendarmerie* to round these people up, Harzig?'

'Nothing,' Harzig answered calmly.

'*Nothing!*'

'Yes, *Herr General,* so far I have not reported my findings to anyone except yourself.'

'In three devils' names, why not, man?' Priess exploded. 'Those damn *Amis* might strike at any moment and where would we be then?'

Harzig took his time before he answered. Outside in the other office, the General's elegant adjutant was saying in an affected Prussian voice, 'But one can't expect a German officer to survive on a litre of watery pea soup a day and half a can of boiled horse, can one?' Priess frowned severely, but he said nothing; he was too intent on Harzig's reply.

'Well, General, if I could have another moment of your precious time to explain, the situation in Metz is like this. We have three divisions to defend some twenty-five square kilometres of territory. The ground is rugged and favours the defender, as you know. As long as Fat Hermann — excuse me, er Reichsmarshal Göring's fly-boys keep us supplied, we can hold out here indefinitely —'

'Yes, yes, Harzig,' Priess waved his hand at the Gestapo man in irritation, 'I know all that. But what has it got to do with these *Amis* wandering around somewhere behind our lines, eh? No, Harzig, I want action — *now*. You can talk later.' His mind made up, General Priess reached out to pick up the ivory-handled elegant French phone on his desk.

In other circumstances Harzig would never have dared to do what he did. But the plan that had been forming in his mind ever since he had left Wanda was too good to be spoiled by hesitation. 'No, General, bear with me another moment,' he said firmly, placing his grubby, nicotine-stained paw on the General's well-manicured hand. 'Let me finish, please.'

Priess withdrew his hand from the phone. 'All right, Harzig, but speed it up for God's sake.'

'Well, as I was saying, General, we can probably hold out here for a very long time. But that is really a defensive role and I am sure both the High Command and you personally, *Herr General*, would like to see us doing something more active for Folk, Fatherland and Führer?'

'But how? All I've got is a burnt-out SS division, an untried bunch of seventeen-year olds in the People's Grenadier Division and a lot of middle-aged cripples — stomach cases, heart cases, arse cases too, for all I know or care,' he snapped angrily. 'How can I attack with troops like that under my command? Talk sense, man, will you?'

Harzig smiled pleasantly, but his eyes did not light up. This was the moment he had been waiting for ever since he left Wanda. Now he must convince the heavy-set General with the fanatic's eyes.

'Yes, I understand and sympathize with your position, *Herr General*. But what if we could use those *Amis*, who are now somewhere behind our lines for an offensive role?'

Priess looked at him, as if he had suddenly gone crazy. 'Heaven, arse and twine, man, what are you talking about?'

'Well, General,' Harzig replied calmly, unmoved by the other man's sudden outburst, 'we all know that that cowboy General of theirs, Patton, has his headquarters at Nancy. To be exact, in the barracks at the Rue du Sergent Blandau, not far from Place Stanislas.' He smiled like a conjuror producing a rabbit from his top-hat, his mouth suddenly gleaming with gold teeth. 'We of the Gestapo have full details of the location of his office, his habits, the address of his private quarters in the town — everything. After all, there are many Frenchmen who have not lost their faith in German invincibility. And if the faith is weak, well there is always money.' He made the Continental gesture of moving his thumb and forefinger, as if he were counting notes. 'So, *Herr General*, it struck me this morning when I discovered that wrecked *Ami* armoured car and realised that a force of them had passed through our lines, that we might use them for —'

Swiftly he explained his bold plan, while SS General Priess listened in silence, his protests dead now, his enthusiasm for the fat, disgusting Gestapo man's scheme growing by the second. Immediately he realised its potential. If it came off, it would put Skorzeny's bold rescue of Mussolini in 1943 completely in the shade. Doors would be opened to him everywhere. Perhaps he would exchange his present worn-out corps for an army? The Führer was inevitably generous to those who pleased him. Hadn't Skorzeny's career since 1943 shown that? As a mere colonel he had the Führer's ear when field marshals had to wait for days for an audience.

Suddenly Priess realised that Harzig was finished and was staring at him expectantly. With an effort of will, he pulled himself out of his splendid reverie of being resplendent with honour, glory and fame and said, 'Harzig, you are a genius, a damn genius, to think up something like that!'

The Gestapo man beamed happily, 'Thank you, General. I had an idea you wouldn't find my little plan totally without merit.'

'Harzig, you have my full authority to carry it out as you have planned. Before you go, I'll get that idiot of an adjutant of mine to give you written authority from me that you are in full charge of — what did you call it?'

'*Operation Cuckoo*, General.'

Priess laughed. 'Apt, very apt indeed, Harzig. And be assured, my people will give you every assistance. I'll see that you get priority number one.' His smile disappeared suddenly and he looked at Harzig, as if he were seeing the shabby cop for the very first time. 'But tell me, Harzig, what are you doing this for? After all, they could well be desperate men. You might be in some danger, you know.'

'It is my duty, *Herr General*,' Harzig replied, dropping his eyes to his big dirty boots, as if he were suddenly embarrassed.

Priess was not fooled. In spite of his wooden expression which gave him the look of some ex-regular NCO who had worked up to officer rank by dint of sheer, plodding effort, he was a shrewd, highly intelligent commander who had always had an eye for the main chance. He knew human nature. 'Come on, Herr Harzig,' he chided the other man softly, 'we're not in a convent here and that's not green in my eyes, you know,' he tugged at the corner of his right eye in the German gesture of disbelief. 'Everybody wants something. What do you want? Promotion, decorations, money?'

Harzig hesitated and then it came out. 'General, I'm not a coward,' he said hurriedly, 'not much of one that is. But I must get out of Metz — *soon*.'

'Why?'

Harzig swallowed suddenly, realising as he formulated his answer just how alarmingly true his own words were, 'General, if the *Amis* ever do take Metz and we are captured, you as an officer will suffer the indignity of a POW camp. Unpleasant but comparatively harmless. But do you know what my fate will be, *Herr General*?'

Priess shook his big heavy head.

'They'll hand me over to the Frogs and I know what they'll do.' He looked down at his pudgy hands, as if he could see the blood of the tortured Frenchmen with which they had been stained so often in these last years, *'They'll tear me to pieces — slowly!'*

It had been his French *petite Amie*, who had finally decided him to approach Priess with his plan. After their usual midday session in her dark little room in the *maison de passe* in Metz's crumbling red light district, she had dropped the bloody whip and reclined on the bed to let him do what he wanted. She lay on her back, black-booted legs apart, staring at the flaking ceiling in boredom. When he had finished and lay beside her, his fat face buried in a dirty pillow, his heart beating like a triphammer gone crazy, she said in a hoarse masculine whisper, which thrilled him even now after a year of her 'special treatments', 'I've had a nose full, Fritz — a shitty nose full — and I want out.'

Sore but very relieved, he had turned round painfully and stared at her raddled, hard face, 'What do you mean, Wanda *cherie*?' He had attempted to take her wrist, but she had torn it away hastily.

'I'm sick of the siege, of Metz, you Fritzes, the *Amis*, the whole shitty war — and I want out!'

Angrily she had jumped from the bed and swung the bloody lash against the tall, high-heeled boot laced up to the knee, her big white breasts trembling like puddings in the cups of her black-satin corset, as if they might pop out at any moment. 'I've made plenty of money. You too, Fritz. So,' she had shrugged expressively in the French fashion, 'why not get out before those *sales cons* of the Maquis get us.' She had swung round, the bloody snake-hide whip held aloft threateningly, and he had shuddered in delicious anticipation. But she had had other more real threats in mind. 'Because when they do take Metz, you know what they will do to people like us? It won't be just playing like now. Oh no, my fat Fritz friend, they will teach both of us of what special treatments really are.' She had laughed harshly and had looked down at his ugly white body contemptuously. 'Then the *real* games will start, believe me.'

'But Wanda, darling,' he had protested. 'We can't get out. Metz is surrounded. Be sensible — there is no possible escape route.'

'Not for a Fritz like you, perhaps. But Wanda will find a way. I've got a suitcase of silver and I've got a body.' She had run her hard hands down her plump body, forced into the tight satin corset and glistening crêpe-de-Chine panties, which threatened to split every time she bent down. 'We of the horizontal profession can always charm you male pigs into doing what we want you to do, *eh*?' She had cracked the whip menacingly.

'Yes, yes, Wanda,' he had replied hurriedly. 'But all the same, you must be sensible and face up to facts. We are surrounded here. There is no way out.'

'Then find one, Fritz,' she had snarled, 'and soon! Otherwise, your little Wanda will start making arrangements of her own, *compris?*'

That final threat had made up his mind for him.

For nearly ten years Harzig had thought he was impotent. His wife Klara's skinny charms, clad mostly in thick red flannel, had not raised a spark of sexual desire in him for many a year and after a time the routine boredom of the average whore he had bought to replace Klara's failing power of attractions had begun to repel him. Wanda, the tall heavily-built Frenchwoman with the husky whisper and the delightful black whip, had rekindled the old desire in him. Suddenly at the age of fifty-five, he had undergone a second, if somewhat more complicated and painful, sexual youth, under her skilled tuition. Now he could not do without her. He was hooked on her and the new perversions she had brought into his boring loveless life, as if on some very potent and exciting drug.

Thus Operation Cuckoo had been born. Yet now, as he walked slowly across the cobbled courtyard of Priess's HQ to his waiting Volkswagen jeep, *Kommissar* Harzig realised the task he had set himself in return for an air passage back to the *Reich* for himself and Wanda would not be easy. It would not be too difficult to find the *Amis*. How could they hide the ten or so vehicles he estimated they had with them, inside a garrison of nearly one hundred thousand German troops? No, no, that wouldn't cause too many problems. Give him twenty-four hours — at the most — and they would be safely locked up in the cellars of the Gestapo HQ facing the towers of the old city gate *la Porte des Allemands*.

It was what would come next that would present difficulties. How would he convince a group of men, who were undoubtedly very brave — otherwise they would not have volunteered to undertake this bold mission — to carry out the task that he had planned for them? The threat he would have to use had to be powerful — very powerful. Abruptly the delightful vision of Wanda's blood-stained whip flashed before his mind's eye and he realised immediately, how he would have to do it. That method always worked.

As *Kommissar* Hans Harzig crashed home first gear and started to nose the clumsy-looking, camouflaged Volkswagen out of the HQ he felt suddenly happy. In twenty-four hours' time the *Amis* lurking somewhere within the great fortress city would be in his power and then he would teach them what fear really meant...

CHAPTER 3

It had been Limey's idea that first night. Cautiously the crew of Old Baldy had approached the shattered freight yard on foot when they had been hit by the terrible stench, which smelled as if all the sewers in the world had been opened.

'Christ almighty!' Triggerman had exclaimed, forgetting the danger of their position, 'did you spill ya guts, Dutchie!'

'No, I goddam didn't, Triggerman. Now knock it off, will ya,' Dutchie had replied indignantly. 'The stink is coming from over there — from them freight cars.'

They had worked their way through the mess of shattered, grotesquely twisted locomotives and flat cars grouped around the ruin of a locomotive shed, until they had come to a line of freight cars from which the horrible stench emanated. Gasping for breath, Wheels had cried, 'Holy mackerel, Major, get a load of that. *Coffins*! The thing's full of Kraut stiffs!'

For a few moments they had stood there, fingers gripping their noses to keep out the stink, eyes round and staring at cars stacked seven feet high with soft-wood coffins. Then Limey, as always the quickest off the mark, had stepped forward and rapped the first coffin with his knuckles. There was a sharp hollow sound. 'Why, sir, they're empty,' he had cried.

And so they had been. They had pried open a couple and soon proved that. 'But where the hell's that sodding pong coming from?' Limey had demanded.

In the end they had found its source. Attached to the end of the line of freight cars, bearing the empty coffins, there were two other cars. From the corner of the first one, an odious, evil-smelling yellowish liquid was oozing from a half inch crack in the wooden planks and the wind was carrying that terrible odour across the trainload of empty coffins. Quickly Limey, holding his nostrils with one hand, had reached in the other hand and grappled in the darkness until he had found what he sought. 'Here, yer are,' he had grunted in disgust, pulling it out, 'cor fuck a duck! A sodding rotten head o' cabbage!' The cause of the stink had been a consignment of cabbages, which had been caught in the air attack that had brought the German train's progress to a sudden and final halt here at the suburban freight station.

It had been a few minutes later that Limey had put his plan forward to Major Hardt, worried about where he was going to hide his T-Force before dawn broke, which wouldn't be long. 'Sir,' he had exclaimed excitedly, 'I've got an idea.'

'Well, look after it well,' Hardt had replied gloomily, 'it's not given to us all to have ideas at this time o' the morning.'

'No, sir, I'm serious,' he had persisted, his usual cheeky Cockney grin gone. 'In a couple of hours it'll be daylight and we'll have to have a place to laager by then, or old Jerry'll really have us by the short and curlies proper.'

'Yeah, yeah, you don't need to draw me a picture, Limey. I read you okay.'

'Okay, sir, I've got that hiding place for us.'

'Where?'

'Here,' Limey had announced proudly, 'Well, you know sir how shit-scared of getting diseases the Jerries are? I mean you'd see their POWs in Africa always washing themselves all over in case they'd catch something. All over and every day,' he had repeated, as if such cleanliness was hardly believable. 'I mean it ain't natural, is it?'

'Get on with it, Limey, willya!'

'I was just going to, sir. Well, seeing the Jerries are scared of catching something, let's really scare the buggers shitless. With that ruddy pong and them coffins, it'd be easy.'

'What do you mean?'

'We'll make this place into a typhus area. Put up little signs everywhere right round the yard and hide up in that engine shea over there. It's big enough to take all our vehicles.'

Hardt had seized the idea enthusiastically. Limey, of course, was right. The Germans did have this pathological fear of disease. Their prisoners always had their pockets and ammunition pouches full of pills of all shapes and sizes to be taken against obscure diseases. He had often thought that it was no wonder the pre-war German pharmaceutical industry had been so prosperous. Thirty minutes later a dozen of the empty coffins had been broken up, a crude skull and cross-bones painted on them (with paint found in the shattered locomotive shed) and the sinister words — '*Achtung* — *Typhus-gefahr! Nicht Betreten!*' An hour later they were safely settled in the big ruined shed, the area effectively sealed off by the frightening signs and even more frightening stench of rotting 'corpses'.

That had been the night before. Now apparently safe in their secret camp within the enemy lines, Major Hardt planned the next move. Facing the men squatting on the floor of the big shed with its glass roof shattered into a gleaming spider's web in the thin rays of the yellow morning sun, he briefed them on what he was going to do. 'So it appears, fellers, that we're comparatively secure here. Touch wood.' He tapped his head and they smiled faintly. 'But we can't push our luck too far, can we?'

'Yeah, you can say that again,' Triggerman snarled, his olive face as sour as ever.

'Knock it off, you jerk!' Big Red barked, his face flushing an even deeper red, as it always did when he had any dealings with the ex-Mafia man. 'Let the Major get on with his talk, willya.'

'Thanks, Red. Okay, this is the situation. We're through the Kraut lines, as you know, and holed up to the south-east of Maizières on the road to Saint Rémy. From there it's only a matter of a couple of klicks to Metz itself. But then we'd be faced with the Kraut second defensive line, running from just north of a place called Wippy — below Saint Rémy — right into Metz itself, down to the bridges across the Moselle. According to Colonel Koch of Army Intelligence.' He hesitated a moment and let the information sink in. 'Now we've got to get through that second line of defence before we can approach the Führer Battery and my guess is that the best way to do it is via Metz itself.'

'But that'll be pretty tricky, sir,' Wheels objected. 'The Krauts'll have patrols out.'

'Sure, I know that, Wheels. But there are still plenty of French civvies inside the town, whereas they've been evacuated from the surrounding countryside. So if we tried to work our way around Metz, we'd stick out like a sore thumb. We'd be picked up pretty damn smartish.'

'But Jesus, Major,' Triggerman objected, 'What kinda deal is that?' Contemptuously he ran his fingers down his stained combat jacket. 'How far do you think we'd get in these duds before the Krauts jumped us?'

'But we won't be wearing those duds,' van Fleet interrupted in his soft, sinister way, a faint smile on his thin lips, but with no answering light in the dark eyes gleaming behind his steel-rimmed GI glasses. 'Will we, Major?'

Hardt shook his head slowly, almost as if he were reluctant to carry on. 'No, we won't, van Fleet.' He raised his voice by an effort of will. 'You see fellers, we've brought enough civvies along with us to rig out the crew of Old Baldy for a preliminary recon of the Kraut positions down there in Metz…'

His voice trailed away, as he waited for his crew's reaction to the announcement.

But Big Red did not give them an opportunity to react. 'When do we move out, sir?' he snapped, his two hundred pounds of brawn and muscle tensed to silence any objection to the bold plan.

'Tonight, Red. At dusk.'

In front of his listeners, Dutchie clutched his rosary more firmly in his big dirty hands and breathed, 'Brother, this is where the shit really hits the fan!'

But the rest of the crew remained silent, preoccupied with their own thoughts. And a grim-faced Major Hardt, standing looking down at them, knew what those thoughts were. If they were caught in civilian clothes behind the Kraut lines, there would only be one way out for them: the short walk at dawn, the last cigarette before the blindfold was wrapped round their eyes and then the thunder of the firing squad. Shot as spies…

CHAPTER 4

Metz was dying.

That afternoon the American dive bombers had attacked once more. Scores of them, falling from the sky at four hundred mph and levelling out at the very last moment, as the myriad deadly little black eggs started to pour from their metal bellies. Time and time again. Hour after hour.

Now they had gone. But as the smoke began to drift away, the cautious little group of Americans in shabby civilian clothes could take in the stark horror of the bombed city as they got closer and closer to the centre. Whole blocks had been rubbed out. Where once there had been prosperous eighteenth century villas, there was nothing but piles of grey, smoking rubble, interspersed by scores of fresh, brown-earth craters and grotesquely twisted, glowing girders.

'Jesus wept,' Limey whispered to Hardt, 'the Brylcream boys really did give this place a proper pasting.'

Hardt nodded but said nothing. Grimly he took in the terrible scene of death and destruction. For the first time he realised what it must be like to be on the receiving end of a mass Allied air attack.

'Look out, sir!' Red yelled, forgetting Hardt's warning not to be too loud. The Major started back. Just in time. Like the sound of a great wave breaking on the Pacific coast, followed by a long drawn-out hiss, a wall directly in front of him came crashing down. A thick cloud of dust engulfed him. He staggered out of it, coughing and choking. A head, still encased in a white, ridged French helmet, rolled to a stop at his feet.

Dutchie Schulze crossed himself hastily. 'For crying out loud, sir,' he exclaimed, 'let's get the hell outa here!'

'Yeah,' Triggerman added his plea too, 'before they throw the rest of it at us.' He drew back his foot like a soccer player and booted the helmeted head into the debris-littered gutter.

Dutchie shuddered and turned a greenish white.

But in spite of the bombing and the nightly artillery barrage which would start soon, there were civilians around. Like primitive cave dwellers, they now emerged from their shelters and cellars to scavenge for food, fuel and, most precious of all, water. Handkerchiefs and rags tied around their mouths against the ash and soot which still rained down from the burning suburban villas, they started to flood the narrow cobbled streets of the old city around the stark Gothic outline of the medieval cathedral.

And there were German soldiers everywhere too, snatching a few hours from the grim reality of the front to enjoy the cheap escape offered them by the women who now stood in the doorways on both sides of the shabby streets. Their dyed black hair hanging to their shoulders, shaggy fur jackets covering thin, cheap flowered dresses, they posed there, legs spread apart, little torches pressed against the pits of their skinny stomachs to illuminate their pathetic sexual charms, whispering huskily with bored professional concupiscence, '*Ficki-ficki, Deutscher Soldat? Du ficken? … Zigaretten … Fleisch…?*'

The young men in field-grey did not hesitate. Cigarettes and cans of 'Old Man', as they called their standard meat ration, reputedly made of dead pensioners, changed hands rapidly. The torches were extinguished and they enjoyed their fleeting moment of rapture in the quaking, moaning darkness, clutching the whores as they crouched there in the doorways.

'Oh lovely grub,' Limey moaned softly, 'one great big open-air knocking shop, Major. *Grr*! Let me get out of here or I'll be walking with a sodding limp for the rest of me natural days.'

Hardt grinned and pushed his way through a couple of young SS troopers haggling with three whores about the price. Silently he thanked God for the civilians and the whores. They made the presence of Old Baldy's crew in the blacked-out streets less conspicuous.

Slowly they made their way through the besieged city, coming ever closer to the Moselle, where Hardt knew they had to bear right and continue westwards along the bank of the river. They couldn't risk trying to cross one of the bridges in case they were guarded by sentries, wanting some kind of identification from them. That would be fatal. They passed the first bridge — a casual line of French civilians, out to find a few odd scraps of food for yet another day of war. Idly the sentries, in their little red-and-white striped boxes, watched them as they wandered by, their shoulders bent, as if to acknowledge the fact that they belonged to a beaten people. They cleared to the second one in the same fashion.

They started the long climb to the heights from which they could overlook the battery, which was their target. Again they found themselves in the suburbs: grim, grey and industrial, shattered factories and workshops long knocked out of action by the almost continuous American air and artillery bombardment. Here furtive figures lurked in doorways once more. But this time they weren't selling their bodies; they were selling food. Obviously they had entered the besieged city's black market district. In heavily-accented German and the more rapid, guttural French of Lorraine, the passers-by were offered cigarettes, cans of food, wine, followed by an angry curse when they refused to stop and buy.

'Don't take any notice of them,' Hardt hissed. 'Just keep going as if we've got some specific aim in mind. Keep going!'

Five minutes passed. And another. They were still in the black market district, but there were fewer of the furtive figures now; and Hardt knew why. They were getting very close to the German's second line of defence now, and the front. The rumble of the guns was getting louder by the second and the night sky was split time and time again by the scarlet flashes of the exploding shells. Not even the tough, greedy black marketeers were going to risk their skins in this area for a handful of coarse, German cigarettes.

They came to a crossroads. The main road ran straight ahead, climbing steadily towards Gravelotte and the heights where the old Prussian Guard had once defeated the Imperial French Army one hot August afternoon many years before. Hardt hesitated. Surely, he told himself, the Krauts would have a standing patrol on that road. He made up his mind. It was dangerous to continue along the road. 'Okay, we'll take the side road — the one to the right,' he ordered in a whisper.

Obediently his men followed him. Silently, like grey North American timber wolves emerging from the endless pine forest in search of prey, they slunk into the deep shadows cast by the tumbledown houses. For a few minutes they plodded up the street, their boots seeming to make a devil of a noise in its tight confines; then suddenly the street opened up and on the next hilltop, clearly outlined in the moon which had emerged from the ragged clouds, they could see it. 'The Führer Battery?' van Fleet asked.

'Yes,' Hardt said swiftly, recognising it from the brief glimpse he had had of it during his ill-fated flight with Bright Eyes, 'that's it all right.' He rapped out a quick order and the rest of the crew crouched in the shadows, while he and van Fleet crawled forward and flopped behind a pile of abandoned timber.

To the west, the Battery was well hidden by the thick wood which crowned the hill, but to the east, facing Metz, they could easily make out the converted fort's narrow bottleneck of an entrance: a concrete gateway, dominated by sandbagged positions, which would probably be manned by the place's covering infantry. 'Tough tittie, eh, Major?' van Fleet said, reading his thoughts.

'Tough tittie indeed, Clarry,' Hardt agreed, as he searched the area, picking out the steel cupolas of the batteries which covered the four key forts, the cunningly concealed flak batteries and the machine gun nests, which dotted the eastern side of the hillside. 'A real sonuvabitch to crack.'

He leaned back against the timber and rubbed the back of his hand across his aching eyes, trying to impress the details of the place on his brain for future reference, wondering at the same time how the hell they were going to get into the place and put those great concealed guns out of action.

'It'll be no use trying to take it by a frontal attack on the main gate, skipper,' van Fleet said reflectively, again echoing his thoughts.

'Yeah. You're right there. By the time we'd have broken in, the whole damn Metz garrison would be alarmed. No, that's out for a start.' He rolled over on to his stomach again and took another look at the squat sinister outline of the fortified battery. 'But it's through that damned gate we've got to go. There's no other way.'

'But *how*, skipper?' van Fleet persisted.

For the time being, however, that overwhelming question had to remain unanswered. At that very moment the nightly American artillery barrage started up. There was a sudden dull groaning noise, which rose almost instantly to a baleful, angry scream.

'Incoming mail,' Red bellowed, 'Get them goddam heads of yours down!'

They needed no urging. The next moment the full fury of the bombardment swept over them and crashed down on the suburbs behind in a great wave of manmade destruction.

Vicious purple tongues of flame were leaping up everywhere among the shattered buildings as they hurried back the way they had come. Everywhere bodies lay sprawled out in the abandon of death. The wounded, men and women, writhed in agony on the gory cobbles, crying weakly for help which did not come. In front of them an apartment block collapsed with a great roar. Red glowing sparks flew high into the burning sky. They ran into a side street. Not a hundred feet away, a horse-drawn *Wehrmacht* convoy received a direct hit. Some of the horses went down straight away, their bodies slashed to ribbons by the shrapnel, whinnying piteously as they sank to the cobbles. Others broke their traces. Eyes wide with terror, burning manes streaming behind them, they clattered madly down the street, dragging the shattered carts after them.

'Bugger this for a sodding tale!' Limey gasped, as they doubled back. 'Bad enough the Jerries trying to knock us on without you bloody Yanks having a go at it too!'

But no one was listening. Each and every one of Old Baldy's crew was concentrating on surviving the crazy inferno, springing over the burning debris, shoving aside dazed, wounded civilians, pelting up and down streets which shook wildly under their pounding feet.

Then, as abruptly as it had started, the nightly bombardment stopped, leaving behind it a loud echoing, somehow even more frightening, silence. Gradually the running men slowed down to a trot and finally to a walk. But for what seemed a long time no one spoke, not even Limey. The civilians started looting the newly damaged houses and shops immediately. Like a horde of evil grey rats they swarmed out of the cellars and shelters where they had been hiding during the bombardment, bags and sacks already ready for this nightly exercise. Ignoring the wounded, lying groaning for help in the bloody gutters, they grabbed what they could find — cans, bales of cloth, loaves — and stuffed them in the bags before moving on to the next smoking ruin.

The T-Force men looked at each other with shocked eyes. They have never seen anything like this before — a pack of animals in human form, snarling in the dirt of the gutters for a few trinkets — not even in North Africa. They passed a group of women, crouched over a dead horse, sawing at it like the furies themselves, their hands covered with blood to the wrists, slashing and ripping at it in desperate haste to carry away a piece of the precious meat.

'Christ on a crutch,' Triggerman breathed, 'get a load of them dames!' Even his usually contemptuous attitude vanished at the sight, as he added incredulously. 'Ya wouldn't believe it, if ya didn't see it, would ya, guys!'

Hardt nodded and snapped, 'Yeah, but let's speed it up, fellers. There's going to be trouble soon … I can smell it in the air!'

They quickened their pace, brutally pushing their way through the milling, confused alleys and back streets of the old town near the river. They passed the first bridge and the second. Now the sentries there were alert and at the entrance to the second bridge, a group of young SS men in camouflaged, mottled capes were setting up a Spandau machine gun, as if they expected trouble to start at any moment. They hurried on, strung out in a file on the pavement, hands gripping the pistols hidden in their pockets, in sudden sweating inexplicable apprehension.

They had just reached the crossroads where the road from Maizières merged with the jumbled network of streets of the old city when it happened. The night was suddenly full of the clatter of half-tracks. Whistles blew. Hoarse commands were rapped in German. Torches flicked on — a myriad fireflies — and the German MPS started to close in on the looters from all sides. They had landed right in the middle of a German police raid!

CHAPTER 5

The T-Force men acted like the seasoned veterans they were. As the half-tracks, filled with SS men in their mottled capes, started to grind down the narrow streets in first gear, following the MPs armed with Schmeissers, they turned as one. It was a natural reaction — not too fast, not too slow — the way some petty French looter would react when confronted with the armed power of the German *Reich*. The police continued their progress at the same steady pace, driving the civilians before them like cattle, obviously intending to pen them in the cobbled square up to the right, where papers would be examined and arrests made.

Hardt's mind was racing wildly now. Once the Germans had them in the square and started asking for identity documents, they were finished. They had to make a break for it before then. Frantically his eyes flashed from side to side, looking for some way out, as the MPs herded them and the rest of the frightened civilians towards the square. In front of him a little runt of a man sucked in his breath suddenly. Dropping the heavy sack he was carrying he pushed through the crowd and dived for the nearest wall. With one great desperate bound he sprang upwards, his hands seizing its top.

'*Halt — stehenbleiben!*' a harsh German voice rapped behind them.

The man did not seem to hear. For some reason known only to himself he was not going to fall into the German's hands. Wriggling and squirming mightily he started to draw himself up the wall.

'*Halt oder ich schiesse!*' the same voice ordered.

The Frenchman continued his attempts to climb the wall. Now he had half his body on top. In the same instant the MP opened up with his machine pistol. Bullets cut the night air viciously. Women screamed hysterically. Men flung themselves to the cobbles. Suddenly all was confusion, as the little runt crumpled from the wall, almost sawn in half by the slugs, and hit the pavement with a sickening thud. It was the opportunity Hardt had been waiting for. 'After me — at the double!' he hissed urgently.

Springing over the tense bodies lying everywhere, he pelted for the entrance to an alley on the right. His men ran after him. For a moment the Germans did not react. Then a hoarse voice called something angrily. Next instant a machine pistol chattered. Slugs whined off the wall, sending blue sparks flying everywhere. A fragment of stone struck Hardt on the cheek. He yelped with the sudden pain, but he didn't stop running. Neither did his men. They pelted into the dark alley. Behind them, the German MPs fought their way through the crowd of civilians and the half-tracks increased their speed, gunning their engines in a sudden burst of noise.

For a fleeting moment the pale moon slipped from behind the clouds and flung a thin shaft of silver light on the two men standing at the end of the street. It was only for an instant, but sufficiently long for Hardt to see the gleam of the metal crescent around their necks. They were Kraut MPs!

'*Halt!*' a schnapps-thickened voice, used to giving commands and having them obeyed, confirmed his swift recognition. The moon disappeared again, throwing the narrow alley into pitch darkness once more.

'Keep going,' Hardt gasped.

Behind him Triggerman drew his forty-five. 'To the left, Major,' he snapped hastily.

Hardt did as he was ordered.

'*Halt, sage ich!*' the voice in the darkness commanded again. It was a foolish thing to do.

Triggerman fired, using the voice to guide him. Scarlet flame stabbed the night. Hardt caught a dramatic glimpse of the MP, knees buckling beneath him, hands fanning the air wildly, while his pistol clattered to the cobbles, and then darkness closed in on his death agonies. An instant later Wheels had closed with his petrified comrade. The German staggered back with a scream of absolute agony, as the little ex-cabbie whipped the muzzle of his pistol across his face and blood spurted through his fingers in thick jets. Next to Wheels, Limey jammed his knee into the German's crotch. As he doubled up, trying to scream through the hot vomit which suddenly filled his throat, Limey rammed his kneecap right under the German's jaw. Something snapped. The MP went down instantly, his neck broken.

They ran on.

Behind them a machine pistol opened up with a thin high-pitched scream. Lead stitched a blue pattern of sparks at their feet. Slugs whined off the cobbles everywhere. Triggerman paused for a moment and firing over his shoulder, sent a bullet winging towards their pursuers. An MP skidded to a sudden stop and fell heavily to the wet cobbles. Behind him the driver of the nearest half-track tried to brake in time. Without success. The tracks churned the MP's body into a bloody pulp. Suddenly the air was full of enraged cries and the wild chattering of machine pistols. Triggerman turned and ran on after the others.

They swung round a corner. A high wall loomed up in front of them, to their right.

'Up there — quick, for Chrissake!' Hardt gasped.

Without waiting to see if they had heard his order, he sprang up and clasped the glass-covered, jagged top. His hands felt as if a dozen razor blades had been driven into the palms. But he had no time for the pain. Blood spurting in hot agony, he drew himself up. The rest of the T-Force men did the same. Behind him the noise of their pursuers was getting ever louder, but all the same they were advancing cautiously. None of the MPs wanted to suffer the fate of their comrades.

Dutchie, the heaviest and the slowest of the crew, jumped for the top and missed his hold, yelping with acute pain as the jagged broken glass tore into his palms.

'Jesus, shut up!' Triggerman hissed with rage. 'Get yer fat fish-eater's ass up here!' Ignoring the glass digging into his chest, he leant over and pulled his buddy up.

They were in some kind of a garden, long neglected now and covered with wet weeds. In the darkness Red blundered into a glass cloche. He crunched through it, cursing furiously. From beyond the wall, there was a sudden cry, as their pursuers were alerted by the noise. '*Hier... die sind hierdrueben*' someone yelled in triumph. '*Schnell.*' There was the sound of heavy boots stamping across the cobbled alley.

They ran heavily through the abandoned garden. A gate loomed up. Panting wildly, Hardt flung it open and ducked back inside the garden the next instant. 'Balls!' he cursed angrily.

'What is it, skipper?' van Fleet asked, his chest heaving crazily, as the others blundered to a halt around the garden.

'Half-track ... they've got a half-track up there with a searchlight on its cab!'

'Shit, what now, sir?' Red grunted, 'shall I —'

'No, let me, Sarge.' It was Triggerman. 'The way your mitt is trembling at the moment, all you'd get would be fanny's drawers.'

Red looked down at his big hand holding the pistol in dismay. Triggerman was right. His hand was trembling like an aspen leaf in the wind.

'But,' he began.

'No buts,' Triggerman snapped and pushed by the big NCO. Carefully he eased his way through the gate. Behind them the MPs had still not succeeded in getting over the high wall. But they would soon. He had to succeed with his first shot.

The camouflaged half-track, filled with helmeted SS men, was parked about fifty feet away, its motors ticking over, steadily, while the soldier standing next to the driver ran his searchlight from side to side along the street. The cold white light poked into each deep shadow before moving on again, getting ever closer to the gateway in which he crouched in tense expectation.

Swiftly he straightened up. He brought up his Colt 45 and took aim on the white circle of glowing light, his rigid body still concealed in the shadows. Slowly and very carefully he began to squeeze the trigger, knowing as he did so that he must not miss. He exhaled the last of his breath and fired. The big pistol jerked upwards. The noise of the explosion echoed and re-echoed in the narrow chasm of the alley. Glass splintered loudly. The light went out abruptly. Suddenly they were blinded by the darkness. But they were quicker off the mark than the men in the half-track.

As Triggerman pumped the rest of his magazine into the half-track, enjoying the screams of the men he hit with sadistic pleasure, Hardt sprang to his feet and yelled, 'Come on — across the road!'

A fraction of a second later, they were running madly across the alley, tracer stitching the air in angry confusion all around them, to disappear in the darkness beyond. But even as they made it and the noise of their pursuers began to fall behind them steadily, Hardt, his breath coming in great leathern-lunged gasps, told himself grimly they had left a trail a mile wide behind them...

CHAPTER 6

'There is no doubt about it, *Herr General*,' Harzig said, a happy smile on his round face, 'it was them all right — the *Amis*.'

Priess looked at him coldly, his features set in a stony frown. 'Must you smile like that in three devils' names?' he rapped. 'Grinning like a great ape up a stick! Three of my men were killed last night and another one seriously injured. That is nothing to smile about, Harzig, you know.'

The elderly Gestapo man repressed the joy he felt at his discovery swiftly. A fake look of sorrow crossed his face. '*Natürlich, natürlich, Herr General*,' he said hastily. 'I regret their deaths too — and, believe you me, when the time comes I'll make the shitty Americans pay for it.' He shrugged and his leather coat creaked audibly, 'but as the Frogs say — you can't make an omelette without breaking eggs. Those poor old headhunters died in a good cause, even if they'll never know just how good.'

Priess sighed wearily. 'I suppose, Harzig,' he agreed. 'All right, get on with it. What are your conclusions?'

Harzig responded with unusual eagerness. After last night's bombardment, which indicated that the *Amis* were beginning their softening-up of the defences prior to their final, all-out attack, he wanted to get out of Metz as soon as possible, while the airfield was still functioning. 'I'll take poison on it, sir, it was them all right. The bone-menders found out that the lead taken out of the dead headhunters came from an *Ami* Colt — and Frog black-marketeers don't use that kind of weapon, do they, General?'

Priess nodded his agreement. 'Go on.'

'Well, there were only four or five of them according to the Field Gendarmerie, so I conclude they were a recce party.'

'Possibly, but recceing what?'

'Yes, that's the problem, sir — *what*? They had been in the old city, but there is nothing of importance there, save the black market and the bordellos.'

Priess sniffed. He didn't want to be reminded of Metz's red light district which, although it eased his men's lot, put, on average, fifty of his stubble-hoppers out of action each week on account of what they were wont to call delicately 'a nasty cold at the wrong end.' 'No, there isn't, Harzig,' he agreed. 'Most of our installations lie to the west, if that's what they are after.'

'Well, I'm not going to give myself a headache trying to work out what their target is in Metz. I think it is more important to try to find where they are located at the moment. If you'll allow me, *Herr General*?' Without waiting for Priess's permission, he walked over to the big map of Metz's defences which decorated one wall of the HQ. 'Now, sir,' he began, tapping the map in a pathetic parody of a staff officer giving a briefing. If the situation had not been so serious and the fat little man's plan so promising, Priess would have laughed in his face. Now, however, he remained silent. 'We know the *Amis* broke through our lines — here — at Maizières-les-Metz and that they were spotted — here — last night, north of the river.' He drew a big circle with his pudgy hand, his coat creaking loudly, as if in protest at this unusual effort. 'So, it's my conclusion that they must be hidden in this area.'

'Yes, you could be right, Harzig. And what do you intend to do about it?'

'I'm going to search the area until I find them. Just routine police work sir, that's all.'

Priess stared at him in amazement. '*Routine police work*, you call it?' he snapped angrily. 'Do you know the terrain up there, Harzig?'

Harzig's grin vanished. 'Not really, sir.'

'Well, let me tell you about it.' Now it was Priess's turn to conduct a lecture. 'That area on either side of the Metz-Thionville road is the city's most highly industrialised region. There are factories, mines, workshops, most of them wrecked and abandoned now, every damn where. Why, man, you'd need a couple of battalions to search that area thoroughly. There are a dozen places where your *Amis* could hide. And I simply don't have the men to search for them. I need every blasted single stubble-hopper — anyone who can hold a rifle for that matter — in the line. That cowboy, General Patton, will attack again any day now.'

Harzig held up his pudgy hands, as if to ward off a physical blow. 'I realise that, *Herr General*,' he said in hasty appeasement. 'I realise it too well. But sir, I'm not asking for two battalions of troops, just for two rather elderly specialists who are attached presently to your headquarters and who, if I'm not mistaken, are not exactly rupturing themselves with overwork.'

Priess looked at him sharply. 'What do you mean, Harzig?'

'This, *Herr General!*' Hastily, Harzig explained his scheme for locating the missing Americans in the industrial jungle to the north of the besieged city, while Priess listened in fascinated silence. 'So, don't you see, sir,' he concluded, raising his voice as the *Ami* dive-bombers came zooming in again, 'I'm damn certain they'll report like that and once they do, we'll have 'em, within minutes.'

As the HQ bunker reeled and trembled under the impact of the first bombs and the orders and shouts of alarm started up everywhere outside, Priess nodded his overlarge head in thoughtful agreement. 'By God,' he said slowly, as if he were talking to himself, 'I think you've got it, Harzig!'

While Harzig laid his plans to trap them, the men of Major Hardt's T-Force were not idle either. Under Big Red's energetic command, they prepared to move out of their hiding place, stowing their bedrolls and personal gear in the jeeps, cleaning their weapons and replacing the normal ammunition with tracer, in anticipation of the night action to come. As Hardt commented to van Fleet, a worried frown on his face, while the two officers watched the men go about their preparations: 'They'll be on to us soon, Clarry. Then you can bet your bottom dollar that they put two and two together and come up with five.'

'How do you mean, skipper?' van Fleet asked, telling himself that he had rarely seen the Major so worried as he was now.

'I mean the wrecked Churchill and those damn Kraut cops we killed last night in Metz. They must have tumbled to the fact that we're somewhere behind their lines, and they'll be coming looking for us soon, if they aren't doing so already.'

'But skipper,' van Fleet protested. 'How the Sam Hill are we gonna get into that battery? There's only one entrance. And you know we're not strong enough to bull our way in — we simply don't have the necessary muscle.'

'Okay, okay, van Fleet,' Major Hardt snapped angrily, 'you don't have to goddam well lay it on with a trowel! I know, I know. At the present moment all I'm concerned with is getting T-Force out of this place.'

'But where are we going to hide out, if we leave here, skipper?'

'You remember that little road on the other side of Metz, van Fleet, overlooking the battery?'

The Lieutenant nodded and fumbled unnecessarily with his steel-rimmed GI glasses.

'Well, did you notice that wrecked workshop to the left of that place where we laid up?'

'Can't say I did, skipper.'

Hardt frowned in irritation. 'Well, take it from me there was one — and my guess is that it would take our jeeps comfortably enough.'

'But how are we gonna get through the Krauts in Metz, skipper?' van Fleet asked urgently. 'They're everywhere down there and even one of those cripples from a Stomach Battalion would recognise an American jeep filled with GIs quick enough.'

Hardt smiled suddenly, for the first time since they had returned from their mission to Metz and he had had his hurried little conference with Dutchie and Triggerman. 'I agree, they'd recognise us straight away,' he began slowly. 'But you see I have thought of a little scheme for getting us through, even if they do recognise us.'

Van Fleet looked at him, puzzled. 'How do you mean, skipper?'

But before Major Hardt could explain his cryptic statement, an imposing figure thrust his way into the entrance of the ruined locomotive shed, a Schmeisser machine pistol clasped in his hands. '*Hände hoch — alle,*' he commanded with frightening suddenness. '*Los — wirds bald!*'

Van Fleet's heart sank. Hardt had been right. The Germans had found them all right. Slowly his hands began to creep into the air and then all around him the men of T-Force were laughing and the 'German' was crying, 'Caught you guys with ya drawers down that time, didn't I?'

Van Fleet breathed out a sigh of deep felt relief; the man in German uniform was no other than Dutchie Schulze!

'You see, fellers,' Hardt explained to his men a little later, after the jeeps were packed and their personal weapons were carefully hidden beneath the bedrolls or about their bodies, 'there is no other way we're gonna to be able to do it if we're gonna get within a striking distance of that battery. Naturally the Krauts in Metz wouldn't exactly welcome us with open arms as we are. So', he grinned, 'we're going in as prisoners of war under the guard of those Krauts over there,' he indicated the half a dozen GIs dressed in the German uniforms, which Dutchie and Triggerman had taken from the German dead, 'commanded by *Sergeant* Dutchie Schulze, who will be temporarily resuming the nationality of his forefathers.'

Schulze looked at his big jackboots sheepishly, suddenly a little red in the face at the instant promotion and the fact that he was the centre of attraction for a moment.

'So, we leave the heavy vehicles here, go in the jeeps at dusk. And remember if we're stopped, let Dutchie do the talking — he speaks the lingo — and look nice and tame, as befits a bunch of guys who have suddenly become Kraut POWs. Okay?'

'Yeah,' Big Red thundered, clenching his ham like fists and feeling obviously he had to lend weight to the Major's words. 'And don't none of you jerks forget it. Because if I find any of you lugs looking tough, I'm gonna feed him a knuckle sandwich there and then!' He glowered at the men of T-Force threateningly.

A moment later his threatening look changed to one of red-faced surprise when his words were greeted by a howl of laughter. He turned to Hardt. 'What did I say, Major?' he exclaimed, in bewilderment.

Hardt shook his head, and fought back his smile. 'Forget it, Red, forget it…'

The rest of that day passed with leaden, uneasy slowness while they waited for dusk, for Hardt was not prepared to risk the effectiveness of their 'German guards' during the daylight hours. But finally the sky started to turn an ashen grey and the shadows began to slide over the war ravaged French countryside like evil black crows and an anxious Major Hardt knew it would soon be time for them to move out.

It was about then that he called Limey over to the command jeep and gave him his orders. 'Limey,' he announced, 'we're going to break radio silence. I want you to signal General Patton's HQ.'

Limey's usual good-humoured grin vanished at once.

'That's a bit dicey isn't it, sir?' he said quickly. 'The Jerries are sodding hot on the old radio detection.'

'I know, Limey. But it's a risk we've got to take. I need help from the General.'

Limey nodded his understanding. Without any further objection he swung himself behind the big radio, which was his pride and joy. 'Okay, sir,' he snapped, the complete professional now, 'but try to make it short and sweet so that they can't get a fix on us.'

'I'll do my best, Limey. Okay, here we go.' Swiftly Major Hardt read the message he had prepared from the scrap of paper in his hand. '*Intend to attack position tomorrow pm.* STOP … *Request air support as cover.* STOP … *Own position roughly…*' he read out the grid co-ordinates while Limey spoke swiftly into the mike, adding finally, '*Wish me luck, Hardt.* STOP.'

Limey breathed out hard and took off the earphones. 'You can bloody well say that again, Major,' he said and wiped the sweat from his face.

'Say what, Limey?'

'Wish me luck,' the little Cockney growled, as he tucked the earphones away beneath the set and flung the tarpaulin over it, we're ruddy well gonna need it, if you ask me.' Hardt grinned but said nothing. Thirty minutes later the convoy of jeeps began to edge their way cautiously on to the main Maizières-Metz road. They were on their way.

CHAPTER 7

'*Cochon*!' Wanda said thickly, a *Gauloise* glued to her fat lower lip, her bored eyes staring at nothing, 'didn't I tell you to clean them!'

'But Wanda, *Cherie*, I'm trying my best,' Harzig, crouched naked at her booted feet, quavered in fearful but delighted expectation. He raised his brush, black with polish. 'Look your slave has the brush ready —'

'*Merde alors,*' she grunted, not even taking the trouble to look down, 'clean Fritz!' Idly she swung the whip and brought its black lash across his fat white back.

'Ouch!' Harzig yelped and bent to his polishing once more, rubbing the boot brush across her left riding boot as if his very life depended upon it, his whole body trembling with delight.

Wanda stared out of the window, her dark eyes blank of any emotion save boundless weariness. Outside it was beginning to rain again: the thin bitter drizzle which seemed a permanent feature of this damn grey Lorraine countryside. Suddenly she was overcome by a great longing for the glaring white sun and dry yellow-green of her native Provence, away from this miserable northern city and the damn war which seemed to go on for ever.

'Wanda, *Cherie*,' Harzig broke into her reverie, 'would you move your right leg a little so that your slave could — well you know?'

She knew well what he wanted. The fat Fritz pervert wanted to look up between her black silk clad legs. '*Sale con*!' she growled in her masterful manner, 'polish and get it over with.'

She swung her whip again and brought it down across his red-scarred back, hard.

This time his yelp of pain was very genuine. 'Wanda,' he cried in tearful protest, 'that *really* hurt your slave! You know you said right at the beginning that you wouldn't let yourself go unless I asked for it, *Cherie*!'

She looked down at him, her dark eyes blazing with sudden rage. For a moment she was tempted to really give him a whipping. Then she caught herself in time. After all he was of the Gestapo — and she needed him if she were ever going to get out of Metz with a whole skin. Controlling her rage, she flung her whip on to the ancient bed in disgust. '*Idiot*,' she cursed, 'stop now — I'm no longer in the mood.'

'But Wanda!' he protested.

'Hold your big Fritz trap!' she snapped in disgust, and, lighting yet another *Gauloise* from the stub glued to her bottom lip, she flopped onto the bed. It squeaked in protest under her weight.

Crouched on his knees, Harzig looked up at her plump body in dumb animal reproach, then silently began to gather up the gear — the brushes, the clothes, the polish — they used during his 'special treatments'. Finally he had them packed away under the *commode* and turned to look at her with a worried sulk. 'What has your slave done wrong?' he asked hesitantly.

'Oh, shut up with that slave rubbish,' she answered angrily, puffing moodily at her cigarette. 'The situation is too serious for pleasure. In the old city they say that the Americans are going to launch their final attack at any time. And what are you doing about getting us out before they do?' She pouted her lips in the French gesture of disgust. '*Nothing*!'

'But I have, Wanda,' he protested hastily. 'You know I would do anything for you. Any day now, any hour now even, you and I will be flying from this damn city, courtesy of the German *Luftwaffe*.'

She turned slowly and looked at him curiously, as if she were seeing him for the first time. 'Courtesy of the German *Luftwaffe*?' she echoed his words.

He smiled at her proudly, taking in her delightful body with the red-painted nipples peeping shyly out of the black cups and the gorgeous stretch of ivory-white flesh between the black tops of her stockings and the red frills of her suspender belt. 'Yes, you see I have discovered that there are some Americans behind our lines.'

'So?'

'So, darling Wanda,' he grinned suddenly at his own cunning, 'I decided those same Americans would provide *Kommissar* Harzig and his delightful French friend with a one-way ticket out of Metz. You see this is what I suggested to the Commanding General...' Swiftly he explained the scheme he had put forward to Priess and when he was finished he could see that she was convinced as the SS General had been, though he did not notice the slight look of reserve in her dark French eyes. 'Now then,' he concluded, 'what do you say to that, Wanda, *Cherie*!'

She pouted her lips in fake passion. 'Come over here, my darling, and I will show you,' she breathed huskily.

Harzig needed no second invitation. He ran to the bed, his greedy hands running madly up and down her ample body, raining kisses on her breasts, her mouth, her neck, while she stroked his thinning hair, as if she were trying to soothe some over-excited pet dog, which had just seen a particularly juicy bone.

Finally he was ready. She cupped it with one hard, reddened hand, as if it were a very precious growth. 'Ah,' she breathed, 'my little Casanova is ready so quickly.' With a well calculated sigh, she parted her plump legs. He thrust his hungry hands under her buttocks.

'Climb on me now, my little slave,' she ordered, her dark eyes intent on his steaming crimson face.

'*Ja … ja … Wanda,*' he gasped urgently and raised one dimpled hairy knee prior to mounting her. But it wasn't to be. Just as he settled his flabby stomach comfortably in the warm, sweating cradle of her black-clad legs, a frantic hammering came at the door of her room and an excited voice was calling out in German, '*Herr Kommissar… Herr Kommissar,* are you there?… We've located them… *Herr Kommissar…*'

Their journey through the blacked-out Metz was uneventful. Just outside the suburbs to the north, they had met a column of marching men — infantry moving into the line with that weary gait of infantrymen the world over. Immediately Hardt had nudged Wheels to slow down and as they had passed, Dutchie had leaned out of the side of the cab to cry angry insults at them for having straggled so far into the centre of the wet, cobbled road. The infantrymen took the curses without a murmur. They didn't even protest when the convoy splashed them in mud as it rolled by.

'Doughboys — always the low men on the totem pole,' van Fleet had commented, almost sympathetically. 'It's the same everywhere, skipper, isn't it?'

Hardt had not replied; he had been too concerned with their situation.

But his concern had been unnecessary. The rest of their journey had been without incident. Even the Third Army's artillery had been silent, which had kept the darkened ruined streets free of nosey German MPs, regulating the mess that usually followed the nightly bombardment.

Now as the first pink flashes on the horizon and angry rumbles indicated that the belated nightly 'hate' was about to start soon, they turned at the crossroads and drove swiftly up the side street the crew of Old Baldy had taken the night before on their recce mission. Swiftly Hardt spotted the abandoned factory workshop or whatever it had once been before the siege. 'That's it, Wheels,' he ordered. 'Up there to the right.'

A few minutes later, Dutchie and Red had battered down the nailed-up door with the butts of their grease guns and the jeeps were beginning to move inside. Dimly their blacked-out lights illuminated the place: a long narrow workshop, antiquated lathes that looked as if they might have been used to make the first Model-T Ford lined up on both sides, under a holed ceiling, made of rough-hewn, blackened wooden beams.

'Not exactly a home from home, sir,' Limey commented, stepping neatly out of the icy stream of rain coming down steadily from a hole directly above him.

'No, you can say that again, Limey', Hardt replied. 'But any port in a storm.' He swung round, 'Okay, Red, let's get this thing moving… Bar that door again and see if you can get a look-out on the roof… And no fires or naked lights! Move it!'

Suddenly the shed was full of hectic activity as the T-Force men hurried to carry out Hardt's orders, while Red chased them back and forth like an angry bulldog.

Hardt watched their progress for a brief moment, then he turned to van Fleet, 'Okay, Clarry,' he ordered, 'let's go and have a look-see outside.'

'Wilco,' van Fleet answered smartly.

Together they groped their way the length of the shed and pulled back the evil-smelling old blanket which covered the shattered window at the far end. Hardt put his foot through the rest of the glass and when it had tumbled to the yard outside, he crawled through, followed a second later by van Fleet.

From where they were standing now in the dirty yard, that stank of diesel and stale urine, they could get a fair view of the fort which housed the Führer Battery. Outlined by the pink glow of the barrage, they could see the outside wall where it abutted to the hillside and two of the dull gleaming metal cupolas which hid the guns that they soon hoped to destroy. Then it disappeared into the dark rows of pines marching up the hill like the spiked-helmeted Prussians who had fought over this self-same ground in 1870.

'A very tough baby,' van Fleet breathed, 'and that front gate sure is a beaut.'

'Hm,' Hardt grunted, feeling again the same sense of frustration he had experienced the night before when he had first viewed the place.

'Air shafts — ventilation plant?' van Fleet ventured hopefully.

Hardt shook his head. 'Hardly likely. The original was built in the '90s. And in those days they didn't bother about such niceties.'

'What about the other side of the darned place? There might be an easier entrance there, skipper?'

'Negative. That side is the one covering the other four forts. There'll be no easy means of entrance there, I'm afraid —'

He stopped short, distracted by a sudden metallic clanging noise, mingled with the slow clip-clop of horses' hoofs. The two officers swung their night glasses round, unable for a moment to identify the four objects being towed up the long incline to the battery by the tired nags. Outlined a stark black against the pink sunset, they looked like a series of ancient locomotives from the early days of the Western Pacific, red flames emerging from their long funnels. And then Hardt snapped the fingers of his free hand. 'They're what the Krauts call a goulash cannon,' he explained.

'A what?'

'Yeah, mobile ovens for their hash slingers to cook chow on while they're on the move.'

'I get you, skipper. Chow on wheels.'

'Yeah, kinda.'

For a moment the two of them fell silent while they watched the little convoy's progress towards the gate with interest. As the first horse came level with the great steel gates which barred its way, it swung to the left and moved along the wall. The others followed automatically, without a word of command from the drivers as far as the two silent spectators could judge at that distance. Obviously they had a long-established routine.

The first nag came to a weary halt. For a moment or two nothing happened. Hurriedly Hardt adjusted his glasses to get a better view.

A small steel door, which they had not noticed before, was swinging open in the fort's wall about one hundred yards from the main entrance. A shaft of yellow light cut into the gathering darkness and he caught a glimpse of Kraut fatigue men, who now began to free the first goulash cannon from the traces, while the nag bent to crop the wet grass. Obviously the little convoy had brought up the daily rations for the battery under the cover of darkness.

Slowly and thoughtfully Hardt lowered his glasses and looked at his companion.

Very carefully van Fleet nodded his head. 'Yeah, skipper,' he said, 'If you're thinking what I am — then, *yeah*...'

'*Verdammte Schweinerei!*' Harzig cursed, beside himself with rage that his great scheme had ended so miserably, and rammed his boot against the wheel of the abandoned Staghound. 'Those shitty *Amis* have got away with it again!'

'But they haven't been long gone, *Herr Kommissar*,' one of the Field Gendarmes who made up the hastily assembled raiding party, said. He held up an olive-drab can of hash. 'Still hot,' he announced. 'Wasteful lot of bastards. Half-full still.' He dug his fat forefinger into it and stuck it in his mouth. '*Prima*. Better than the crappy old nag-meat the kitchen bulls feed us.'

'Oh, hold yer damn water,' Harzig snapped. 'I can't think with you opening yer fat lip like that.' He turned away in disgust and forced his tired brain to think, while the middle-aged MPs combed the locomotive shed, filling their pockets with cigarette ends, bars of Hershey chocolate, old cans of *Ami* food.

The *Amis* had a very definite target in Metz, that was for sure, he told himself. The way they had frightened off any prowling stubble-hopper with the typhus signs was proof of that. They were not just ordinary infantrymen; they were experts with a definite purpose in mind. But what was *that purpose*?

He bit his bottom lip and wondered what he should do next. Suddenly his eyes fell on the pale-faced, bespectacled *Luftwaffe* NCO, who had been in charge of one of the disguised radio-detection vans which had guided him to the *Ami* hideout. The NCO had stuck a pin in an *Ami* cigarette end and was smoking it with a look of supreme pleasure on his pale face, as if he were inhaling the pure essence of life itself. 'Sergeant,' he called.

The NCO jumped to his feet, hands automatically reaching for the sides of his ill-fitting grey trousers in the position of attention. '*Herr Kommissar?*'

'I want to talk to you. Come over here.'

Hastily the man dropped his cigarette end and marched over. For a moment Harzig savoured the look of fear in his eyes; the presence of a Gestapo official still had the power to put the fear of death into the average German, he told himself with a pleasurable sense of pride. 'Now you took the message which the two vans used to get a fix on this place, didn't you?'

'*Jawohl, Herr Kommissar.*'

'Well, what did it say?'

Hastily the Sergeant told him. When Harzig heard the numbers of the co-ordinates he felt a sudden surge of hope. 'But that's it,' he interrupted. 'If we can identify those co-ordinates, we'll know their target and we can find them!' he exclaimed excitedly.

The Sergeant shook his head firmly. 'Impossible, *Herr Kommissar.*'

'What do you mean — *impossible?*' he demanded angrily.

'The *Amis* have a different map system than we have — they have different co-ordinates as a result. We'd need one of their military maps of the area to find out where the place is.' He shrugged. 'And we don't have one.'

Harzig bit his bottom lip for an instant. 'But there must be some way of working it out. I mean if we could figure what scale map they normally use —'

'There are dozens of possibilities,' the Sergeant interrupted morosely. 'Take a code expert to work out. Someone with the brain of a —' He stopped abruptly, as if he had just thought of something.

Harzig sensed he knew something. 'What is it, man?' he snapped. 'Out with it!'

'Well, *Herr Kommissar*, in the old days in '42 and '43 when it looked as if … when everyone knew that Germany would win the war, we had a Frenchman with the radio detection team who was a wizard at breaking the Resistance codes. But since the *Ami* invasion, well —' He shrugged and let Harzig draw his own conclusions.

'You mean the Frog bastard got cold feet?'

The NCO nodded. 'Yes, the Professor — that's what we called him because he looked like one — decided it would be better if he became a patriotic Frenchman again. He refused to co-operate with the detection team any more.'

'Is this — er, Professor of yours still in Metz?' he rapped.

'Yes, *Herr Kommissar.*'

'Good, then let's get moving,' Harzig cried, grasping at straws.

'Get moving? Where to?'

'To meet this Professor of yours.' Harzig's little eyes blazed savagely. 'And if he can't decipher those damn coordinates for us — then God help him! He won't live to be a day older!'

The middle-aged NCO shivered suddenly.

PART THREE: THE FÜHRER BATTERY

'I mean this. You, *mein lieber Major*, are to help us to kill that cowboy General of yours in Nancy!'

Kommissar Harzig to Major Hardt.

CHAPTER 1

Major Hardt raised his head carefully. The darkness was almost impenetrable. Yet by using the old trick of bringing his head up from the side at an angle, he could still make out the rough details of the battery: the four domes, the stark outline of the great gate, the bare strip of earth in front of it, cleared specifically to give the defenders an unhampered field of fire in case of attack.

Hardt bit his lower lip. The Führer Battery was a very tough nut to crack indeed. A frontal attack would be sheer suicide. The only way in would be by trickery. If their plan didn't work, he told himself, General Patton would have to wait till 'hell froze over', as he was fond of saying, before the Führer Battery fell.

'Clarry,' he whispered, trying to forget his doubts.

'Skipper?'

'Have you checked?'

'Yeah. Big Red's done a good job of work. He's got the guys in position just to the right of the little door. Without a sound.' Van Fleet chuckled softly. 'I guess they were more scared of Red than the Krauts. Anyway *they're* ready and waiting. Now everything depends on us.'

'You can say that again,' Hardt whispered. 'Brother, if we don't —' He stopped short. He froze into immobility, his heart thudding almost painfully.

'What is it, skipper?' van Fleet hissed.

Slowly, very slowly, the Major indicated the rock outcrop to their left with his hand. 'There!' he mouthed the word almost soundlessly.

Something had moved. Ten or twelve yards away a shadow had detached itself from the rocks. Heavy hobnailed boots scraped on the stone. There was the sound of someone breaking wind followed by that of water splashing on to the ground.

'Kraut sentry pissin', Triggerman, on Hardt's other side, snarled, identifying the figure at once.

The Major nodded urgently, his mind racing as he took in the fact the German sentry carried a machine pistol slung over his right shoulder. One burst from the Schmeisser and the whole damn garrison would be alerted. What was he going to do?

Triggerman seemed to be able to read his mind. As the sentry finished fumbling with his flies and began to plod purposefully down the track towards them, he hissed, 'Shall I take him out, Major?'

Before Hardt could answer, a thin beam of blue light stabbed the darkness. The sentry had switched on his shoulder light in order to see his way down the track more easily. Slowly, inexorably, the thin blue beam came closer to where the crew of Old Baldy crouched on both sides of the muddy track.

Van Fleet reacted first. 'A rock,' he hissed swiftly, 'over there ... behind him.'

Frantically, hardly daring to breathe, Hardt pawed at the wet earth. Mud ... pebbles ... nothing like a decent-sized rock. And the blue light was getting ever closer!

'*Quick*, for Chrissake, skipper,' van Fleet whispered desperately. 'The bastard'll have us in a minute.'

Suddenly Hardt's fingers seized on a fist-sized rock. 'Got it,' he whispered.

'Okay,' van Fleet answered. There was a gleam of silver. He had drawn his favourite stabbing knife. 'Count to three and then throw it.'

'But, Clarry —'

Too late! Van Fleet had already slipped from behind the cover and was crawling up the slope, as noiseless and deadly as a jungle snake.

Hastily Hardt counted to three. He grunted. With all his strength he sent the rock sailing through the darkness. For what seemed an age nothing happened. Suddenly there was the clatter of the rock striking something stony. The blue light wavered for an instant. Then abruptly it was gone, as the sentry swung round to direct it towards the strange noise.

It was a fatal move. A tall shadow rose from the grass. Wraith-like, it padded after the crouched figure of the German. Hardt clenched his fists, hardly daring to breathe. If the Boston socialite didn't pull it off, they'd be in trouble — with a vengeance!

Van Fleet felt a sudden upsurge of that old, old fear which had made him the cold-blooded killer he was. He fought it down desperately. Knowing that if the sentry reacted a fraction of a second quicker than he did he would be a dead man, he deliberately struck the blade of his knife against the rock at his side. The sentry swung round. Van Fleet caught a glimpse of a strained wild young face under the brim of the coalscuttle helmet, then he lunged forward.

The knife plunged through the cloth. It struck the rib cage, careered off and came to a sudden stop as the hilt thudded against the flesh. The sentry grunted. His mouth flopped open stupidly like that of a stranded fish gasping for air. Van Fleet knew no pity. He pulled out the knife. An obscene sucking noise. An instant later he thrust into the man's belly. The knife slid in easily. There was a violent, convulsive exhalation of breath. Van Fleet's hand was suddenly hot and wet with blood. The sentry began to sag on the knife. Hastily van Fleet withdrew it. A moment later the sentry was lying dead at his feet. Van Fleet towered above the German, feeling desperately sick, trying frantically to fight the almost overwhelming desire to throw away the knife and run, run, run...

Finally he pulled himself together. Almost casually he bent down, clicked off the blue light, taking care not to look at the dead man's face, and wiped the blade free of blood on the German's greatcoat. With a grunt, he replaced the knife in its scabbard at the side of his combat boot and plodded back to the others.

'Okay, skipper,' he said, his voice toneless. 'Okay.'

A thin mist was beginning to writhe through the trees where they were lying, tensely expectant, nerves on edge, ears straining for the slightest sound. Hardt looked at the green glowing dial of his watch yet again. If the Kraut hash slingers kept to a schedule, then they should be coming up the track any moment now. He brought his mouth close to Triggerman's ear, 'Pass the word, they should be here soon... And no firing. Okay, got it?'

'Got it, Major — I'm no dummy like that guy Schulze.' As always, Triggerman could not forgo the last word. 'Ya don't have to draw me no picture, Major.' All the same he crawled off obediently enough and carried the message to Dutchie Schulze.

The minutes passed. Hardt was beginning to wonder if the hash slingers would ever come when there was the muffled cough of a tired horse. He stiffened and turned his head to the faint wind so that he could hear better. There was the muted jingle of harnesses, as if they had been wrapped in sacking, and the patient, hollow clip-clop of horses' hoofs. 'Stand by,' he ordered, 'here they come, fellers!'

All around him the crew of Old Baldy tensed, knowing now that the success of the whole bold plan depended upon them. Softly van Fleet drew his knife. Hardt caught a glimpse of the wicked blade, then he concentrated on the little convoy.

A few seconds later, the German cooks came into view. Outlined against the sky, their feet wreathed in mist, as if they were wading through cotton wool, they plodded up the steep track, holding the bridles of the ancient nags dragging the 'goulash cannon' behind them, regular streams of white breath shooting from their nostrils like steam. Surely, Hardt told himself, they *must* hear the waiting men's hoarse breathing, as they waited to spring their deadly trap! But apparently they didn't. They came on unsuspectingly like men who had done this job many times before and expected to be doing it for a long time to come. Born victims, the lot of them, he realised. The cannon fodder of war. Then he dismissed them from his mind. He had other things to do.

Now they had passed the lone oak standing to the right of the muddy track. It was the signal they had agreed upon. Their heads bent in earnest contemplation on their big boots, their helmets coloured a blood-red by the glow thrown out by the tall chimneys of their ovens, the unsuspecting cooks plodded on up the trail.

Hardt sucked in a quick breath, then whistled. Once, twice, three times. The everyday sound seemed somehow very eerie at that time and in that place. The leading German held up his hand abruptly. It was exactly what Hardt had hoped he would do.

'*Now!*' he snapped.

The T-Force men sprang forward. The cooks turned startled and frightened as the shadows descended upon them from both sides of the tracks. A horse whinnied in alarm. '*Was im Himmelsnamen* —' The speaker never finished his cry of alarm. A fist smashed into his surprised face and he went down, as if pole-axed. Next instant all was confusion as the T-Force men attacked.

A whiff of garlic-heavy breath enveloped Hardt. An ox like cook closed with him. Heavy hands grasped his throat. Suddenly his nostrils were full of the stink of the kitchens, as the German, oblivious to the chaotic struggle all around him, grunted with triumph and began to exert pressure.

Stars — red, green and white — exploded in front of Hardt's eyes. Desperately he clawed at the cook's sneering, brutal face. The pressure didn't relax. 'Help,' he croaked. 'For Chrissake, get this bastard off me!'

The cook laughed.

It was the last thing he ever did. Suddenly Limey loomed up out of nowhere. He reacted at once. He brought up his grease gun and rammed the metal butt into the small of the back of the cook's greasy neck. There was the thud of metal against flesh. The cook yelped with pain and relaxed his iron grip.

Gasping for air, Hardt staggered back. Limey dropped his grease gun. Without hesitation he sprang on the German's back. Hanging on there like a monkey, his legs wrapped around the cook's waist, he tugged sharply at the man's helmet. It slipped down the back of his head, the leather strap cutting cruelly into his throat. Limey tugged hard. The German dropped to his knees, eyes wide and bulging wildly, pleading for mercy. Limey gave him none. Swiftly he strangled the man to death until the cook fell to the ground like a broken doll.

'Thanks, Limey,' Hardt said weakly, as all around him the unequal struggle came to an end.

Limey gasped for breath. 'Poor bastard,' he grunted, looking down at the man he had just killed. Then he pulled himself together again. 'But then I never did like sodding cooks — thieving greedy bastards they are, whatever army they belong to.'

Five minutes later, the dead cooks had been bundled off the track and the crew of Old Baldy were dressed in their uniforms, each one of them holding the bridle of an ancient nag.

Hardt took a last look at his men, their faces hollowed out to death's heads in the ruddy light cast by the burning stoves. 'All right,' he ordered softly, 'you all know what to do. We want no snafus on this one fellers. Okay, let's move out.'

Wheels' ancient horse snorted and he started back suddenly. 'Jesus H, Major, how the hell am I supposed to drive this SOB?'

'Put her in first gear and take her up gently,' Limey suggested. 'She's only got a one-horse power engine, you know, mate.'

But no one laughed.

Slowly the little convoy began to climb the height to the grim outline of the fort and what waited for them there.

CHAPTER 2

'All right, you heap of Frog shit — *wake up!*' While the two middle-aged *Luftwaffe* sergeants watched with horror-filled eyes, Kommissar Harzig reached forward and pressed out the glowing end of his cigar on the Professor's blood-stained, unconscious face. There was the stink of burning flesh. The Professor yelped with pain. His eyes flickered open and he was conscious again.

Harzig straightened up and beamed down at the Frenchman, whom he had been torturing for the last half-hour — unsuccessfully. 'That's better,' he said softly, and nodded at the bigger of the two NCOs. 'Give him a snort of that cognac — the cheap one.' He indicated the two bottles they had brought with them to the Professor's ruined apartment, decorated with a few pathetic sticks of nineteenth century furniture. 'The rotgut is good enough for the Frog bastard.'

Silently the *Luftwaffe* man did as he was told. While Harzig made a great play of lighting his cigar once more, the NCO cradled the Frenchman's battered head in his arm and forced a few drops of cognac through his swollen, cut lips.

The Professor coughed thickly and with a weak gesture indicated the NCO should take the bottle away. '*Merci,*' he gasped. '*Merci beaucoup.*'

Harzig stared down at the Frenchman. Although he knew every second was precious if he were going to capture the elusive Americans, he took his time, giving the Frenchman the full benefit of his stare, heavy with menace and superiority. In his time, Harzig had seen plenty of prisoners like the Frenchman: good solid middle-class citizens, who had to learn the hard way that their degrees, their titles, their positions meant absolutely nothing once they were in the hands of the Gestapo. In the end they all crawled as low as any little runt of a sneak thief, who would sell his mother for the price of a glass of beer.

'*Na, Herr Professor,*' he said finally, his voice full of irony, 'would you now be so kind as to give me the information I require?'

The Frenchman, whose collaboration with the Germans in the good years had taken him from his position in some obscure provincial *Lycée* to the chair of applied mathematics at the University of Metz, looked wildly up at his tormentor. 'But I can't … I can't, you must understand that,' he gasped fervently. 'You must!'

'Must I?' Harzig asked cynically.

The Professor did not notice the cynicism. He seized on the words hastily. 'You see, *Herr Kommissar*, the old days are over. If I helped you, I would be in serious trouble with my own authorities.' He licked the spittle from the corner of his split lip. 'And I have to think of my position. You understand that, don't you —'

His words ended in a sudden yelp of pain, as Harzig slapped him across his face — hard — and sent his head reeling against the wall. Behind the Gestapo man, the two NCOs gasped involuntarily and looked at each other, eyes full of shock once more.

'Now listen, you Frog turd,' Harzig snarled, 'I don't give a cold shit for you or your position. Those Maquis fellers are going to have the balls off you whatever you do — probably with one of those blunt cut-throat razors they like to use on your sort. So what are you holding out for. Help us and we'll help you.'

The Frenchman shook his head firmly, his lips pressed tightly together, as if he dare not trust himself to speak.

Harzig made his decision. 'All right, you bastard, you asked for it,' he cried. 'By the time I'm finished with you, you'll be begging me on bended knees to allow you to help us.' He turned to the NCO again. 'You, get me that bidet over there filled up with water. *At the double, man!*'

While the NCO turned both taps on and let the water run into the bidet, Harzig signalled to the other *Luftwaffe* man. Together they grabbed the Frenchman and dragged him across the room, his eyes bulging from his head with horror, already half realising what they were going to do to him in a moment.

The NCO stepped back. 'It's full, Kommissar,' he announced.

'Good.' Harzig seized the Professor by the scruff of the neck. He forced him down so that he stared at the enamel bowl filled with water. '*Non ... non,*' the Professor quavered. Desperately he lashed out with his right foot. Harzig dodged the blow easily. 'All right, you bastard, you've asked for it!' he grunted. The next instant he thrust his head under the water.

Frantically the Professor attempted to free himself, as the water filled his lungs. But the two NCOs were now holding his legs. Squirm and struggle as he might he couldn't free himself. Just as the roaring blackness threatened to overcome him, Harzig dragged him out and let him collapse on the floor, retching agonisingly and vomiting a mixture of blood and water.

'Now he'll talk, Kommissar,' the bigger NCO gasped. 'I'm sure he will.'

'Of course! I'm going to make sure he will. All right, gentlemen, one more time.' He laughed bitterly. 'With feeling, if we can, eh'.

Under Harzig's command, they grabbed the prostrate Frenchman and thrust his head once more into the bidet. The side of his head struck the bowl. Bubbles of air shot wildly from his mouth. Writhing frantically, he tried to escape that terrible grip. To no avail. In his desperate fear, he evacuated his bladder. 'Look the bastard's pissed himself now,' Harzig roared contemptuously, and then he relaxed his hold. 'All right, get him out.'

The two NCOs pulled him out just in time, and when they did, he was screaming through the pink-tinged vomit which filled his mouth, 'I'll do it ... *Anything...*'

Leaning carelessly against the wall, Harzig laughed gruffly. 'Didn't I tell you, gentlemen ... they all break in the end.'

Half an hour later, dressed in a clean shirt, a glass of cognac at his side, the Professor, shaken and pale, pored over the maps laid out in front of him on the table, mumbling to himself as he made swift calculations on the writing pad at his side. 'It's not their usual 1:100,000 sheets,' he announced after a while.

'What does that mean, man?' Harzig demanded, looking over the Frenchman's shoulder and puffing steadily at his cheap cigar.

But the Professor did not seem to hear. Now the torture session seemed forgotten. He was the mathematician again, completely absorbed in the problem. 'Nor does it appear to be one of their 1:500,000 maps,' he muttered, talking to himself as he ran his slide-rule over the map, trying to fit in the two co-ordinates. Suddenly he clicked his tongue in the manner used by French school teachers when they are dealing with a particularly stupid child. 'Of course,' he snapped, 'they're using the 1:20,000 maps we made in the winter of 1939-40. They must have found them in Paris.' Hastily he scribbled several figures on his pad, while Harzig stared down at his bent head in complete bewilderment.

A few moments later, the Professor put his slide rule on the map and drew a neat line across it. He consulted his figures again and then drew another line across it until the two met. Suddenly he looked up, a smile of triumph on his fat, bruised face. 'I've got it,' he exclaimed. 'It's the Mort d'Homme.'

'The what?' The Professor's words were drowned by the crash of XX Corps artillery, which Hardt's radio message had requested, going into action. Harzig ducked instinctively as the villa shuddered like a ship at sea, being hit by a great wave.

'Where?' he asked again, as the first wave of fire rolled across the valley, dragging a loud ringing hollow echo after it, 'Where is it, Frenchman?'

'Mort d'Homme,' he replied, his voice now toneless and exhausted, as if he had just realised for the first time what he had done. 'You Germans call it the Führer Battery...'

'I've got it, Wanda,' Harzig announced jubilantly, as he flung open the door to the whore's room. 'We know where they are — the *Amis*!'

Startled, the aging blonde looked up from the case on the sagging bed which contained silver ornaments and coins, the rewards of her two-year stint in Metz. 'What did you hear, Fritz?' With the heel of his boot he kicked the door closed behind him and cut the thunder of the enemy artillery to a bearable roar. 'The *Amis*, I told you about. Our ticket out of this damned place. Well, I've got them.'

Her eyes lit up. 'Where?'

'The Mort d'Homme. We call it the Führer Battery.'

'Good, good,' she exclaimed, closing the case hurriedly, as if she were already visualising herself entering the waiting Junkers transport which would take them out of the besieged city. 'But what are you doing here, Fritz? Why don't you take them?'

Harzig jerked a thumb like a sausage over his shoulder. 'Because of that. The *Amis* are laying down a barrage between Metz and the battery. It's completely cut off from the city.'

'*Cut off*,' she echoed, her fake smile of triumph and congratulation vanishing from her white-powdered, raddled face as quickly as it had come.

'Don't worry,' he said heartily, noting the look on her face. 'The Führer Battery is defended by the men of the Metz Officers Cadet School, every one of them a former NCO, decorated in action and recommended for Officers' School. They're the cream of the troops here in Metz. Our tame *Amis* won't have much of a chance with those fellows, believe you me, Wanda.' He laughed, showing his gold teeth. 'And even if they did, we'll be waiting for them as soon as that damned firing stops.' He reached in the pocket of his leather coat and took out the bottle of cognac which he had brought from the Professor's. 'Let's have a few drinks, Wanda, eh, *Cherie?*' He looked at her a little pleadingly. 'And perhaps you might let me have one of your special treatments. After all this could well be our last night in Metz together. We should celebrate, don't you think?'

'Yes,' she said, rising to her feet and walking slowly to the cupboard where she kept her whips. 'You might well be right there, Fritz.' For a moment she stood in front of the open cupboard, surveying the tools of her trade. But her mind was far, far away. For Wanda Lejeune was already beginning to make her own plans to escape from Metz and *now* they did not include the fat Gestapo man waiting so expectantly for his 'special treatment'.

CHAPTER 3

'Rations up,' Dutchie Schulze growled in the thick Rhenish accent he had inherited from his German father, born in the shadow of Cologne's Gothic cathedral. 'Let's have yer fatigue men up. We haven't got all night yer know.'

The trim Sergeant, who had opened the little side door nodded. 'All right, all right, hold yer water. You kitchen bulls'll be back in yer nice warm beds down there in Metz soon enough, don't worry.'

'Ay,' Dutchie answered, raising his voice above the roar of the barrage, 'we've got to get back through that shit while you lot are nice and safe behind a couple of kilometres of concrete.'

'Tough,' the NCO said and turned to the white-uniformed fatigue men, waiting in the narrow, yellow-lit passage of the fort, 'All right, make it snappy. Get those goulash cannons unlimbered. Let's see what kind of scorched earth the kitchen bulls have thought up for us tonight.'

Schulze moved to one side, as if to let the two men pass outside to the misty darkness which was split at regular intervals by the savage flame of yet another explosion. 'Over there,' he remarked with feigned casualness and raised his big hand as if to push back his helmet. Instead he moved with sudden, surprising energy. His elbow caught the trim sergeant right under the chin. He went reeling back, gasping frantically for breath, to slam against the wall. In the same instant, Triggerman and Wheels appeared out of the darkness. Before the two fatigue men realised what was happening to them, the T-Force men's heavy sticks descended upon the backs of their bare heads. They fell heavily.

In a flash T-Force swarmed into the passage. The Sergeant was dragged into a convenient cubbyhole near the entrance and trussed up with his own belt and braces, while the two unconscious, bleeding fatigue men were pushed in beside him.

'Okay, Red, get the BAR team in here — at the double!'

The T-Force men who made up the machinegun team needed no urging. Swiftly they moved into the passage from outside, where their comrades were already digging in under the cover of the fort's massive wall, ready to repulse any counter-attack which might be launched after the XX Corps' barrage ended. Under Red's energetic direction they set up their weapons to cover the length of the passage.

Satisfied, Hardt turned to the rest. 'Okay, let's get on the stick, guys!... Clarry, you're with me. Trigger, Wheels and Dutchie, you cover us... You, Red and Limey'll bring up the rear with the explosives.'

'Always the best place in the Lord Mayor's Show,' Limey said cheerfully, 'It's the safest anyhow, unless one of the horses does it on yer.'

But no one had time for Limey's cockney humour now. They were in the heart of the enemy fort, with all of them dressed in enemy uniform, and they knew what their fate would be if they were discovered. They had to move quickly, get the job done and get out. Swiftly, spread out in little groups, as Hardt had ordered, they began to move down the gloomy passage into the depths of Mort d'Homme.

Cautiously, very cautiously, Hardt and van Fleet crossed the cavernous tunnel to the steel ladder let into the concrete wall. On either side of it there were open lifts of the kind the Germans call *Pater Noster*, gleaming metal cages smelling of diesel oil and explosive. 'It's them,' Hardt whispered urgently.

'Shell hoists?' van Fleet queried.

'Right.'

'For the guns?'

Hardt nodded thoughtfully. The hoists would go down to the magazine below, where during any form of action sweating fatigue men, naked to the waist in spite of the October cold, would manhandle the great hundred and twenty pound shells into them for the gunners somewhere above. But at that particular moment he was not interested in the magazine below; his attention was concentrated on the guns in their steel domes.

'Penny for them, skipper?' van Fleet asked softly, his teeth gleaming whitely in the near darkness of the tunnel.

'I was wondering whether they've got anybody on duty up there,' he indicated the domes somewhere in the darkness above them.

'There's only one way to find out,' van Fleet answered, no trace of the fear he felt at that particular moment revealed in his voice.

'Yeah, I know ... I know.' Hardt made up his mind. Swinging round he waved to the rest of the Old Baldy crew crouched in the shadows, weapons at the alert. 'Over here, fellers — quick!'

They moved over. 'All right,' Hardt said, 'the Kraut cannon are up there. Now we don't know whether they've got a crew up there or sentries. But you guys know why we are here. So we've got to go in and find out.'

'How do you mean, sir?' Red asked.

By the way of an answer, Hardt jerked a hand at the two hoists. 'We'll not take the ladder. That would be too obvious. We'll take those wire ropes.' He forced a grin as they stared at him tensely in the gloom. 'I hope you've all got a good head for heights. Because you're gonna need it. Come on.' Without another word, he slung his carbine over his shoulder, grabbed the gleaming metal wire and took the strain. Van Fleet stepped to the next cage and did the same. They began to squirm their way upwards into the darkness of the shafts.

Ten feet … twenty feet … thirty… Panting with the effort, the carbine seeming to weigh a ton on his shoulders, Hardt crawled upwards, wondering whether the shaft would ever end. Another ten feet. And another! The nauseating stink of diesel oil began to grow weaker. He seemed to feel cooler air around his flushed, sweat-lathered face. But there was still no light which would indicate he had reached the top of the shaft. He hauled himself further, the only sound his own strained breathing and that of Limey somewhere in the darkness below him. Would he never come to the opening?

And then there it was — a faint gleam of light ten feet or so above his head. He made a last effort, shinning up the slippery wire as he had once done up the ropes in the gym at the Point, with the immaculate calisthenics instructors bellowing at him from below. A moment later he lay sprawled out on the wet concrete, gasping.

But not for long. Just as Limey reached the top there was a soft hiss, which on any other occasion would have been simply vulgarly funny. Not at this moment though. Now it was a frightening signal of impending danger. ' *Somebody just farted!*' Limey breathed, putting Hardt's fear into words.

'Yeah, up there ahead,' the T-Force commander whispered in reply, carefully unslinging his carbine. 'Down the passage to the right.'

'Sentry?'

'Yes.'

An instant later one shadow detached itself from the darker shadows at the end of the long dripping passage. A torch cut the gloom and caught van Fleet just as he crawled out of his shaft. The sentry reacted instinctively. His free hand flew to the pistol at his waist. But he never drew it. Crouched on one knee, Hardt let him have a wild burst from the hip. Slugs whined off the concrete. But one caught the sentry in the stomach. He screamed thinly and his knees buckled underneath him like a new-born foal. His torch clattered to the ground and went out.

Instinctively Hardt knew the damage had been done already. As the shots echoed and re-echoed hollowly in the tunnel, he sprang to his feet, waving his carbine and shouting — careless of the noise now, 'Come on, you guys! Get your fingers out! Move it!'

Scrambling out of the twin shafts, the rest of his crew followed him as he rushed forward. A man appeared suddenly, as if from nowhere, buckling on his pistol belt. Limey jammed the butt of his grease gun into his face and Triggerman aimed a vicious kick to the side of his face, as he went down on his knees, howling piteously. They ran on. Another German loomed up out of the gloom. Red clubbed him without even stopping. He went down soundlessly. An officer or NCO sprang into the tunnel, blocking their way, pistol at the ready. Van Fleet's knife hissed through the air. The officer's pistol tumbled from nerveless fingers. Terrible gurgling noises came from his throat. Gasping fervently for air and trying to pluck out the knife which reared up from his chest, he hit the ground like a sack of wet cement. One after another they sprang over his inert body, and ran on.

They swung round a corner and skidded to a halt. The corridor turned to left and right and at both ends of the ill-lit tunnel there was the great menacing gleam of the cannons which they had dared so much to destroy. 'It's them all right, sir,' Red gasped.

'Sure,' Hardt agreed. 'Or at least two turrets. The other two must be back the way we came

The sudden burst of machine pistol fire which drowned his words was an indication that there was little chance of getting to them now; the garrison had been alerted. Ricochets zipped off the walls all around them like angry hornets. Hardt made a quick decision. 'Okay, the rest of you, hold the bastards here. Red and Limey — follow me with the explosives.'

Hastily the rest of the crew dropped to the damp floor and took up the challenge at once. The air was full of the snap and crackle of a fire fight. Together with the other two, Hardt went forward to the first pair of cannon. 'Right,' he gasped, 'set 'em up!'

The other two needed no urging. While Hardt pulled out the firing pins and struck each in turn against the wall until the pins themselves broke, Red and Limey kneaded the British plastic explosive into the open breeches and thrust home the ten minute time pencils. Hardt threw their work a swift glance and was satisfied. He nodded his approval and they rose and headed for the next turret. Behind them the fire fight in the tunnel was reaching a crescendo and Hardt could hear an officer shouting, '*Vorwarts ... los, vorwarts, Leute!*' So far, mercifully, no one was following his command, but Hardt knew instinctively that it wouldn't be long before they would try to rush the handful of Americans barring their way. Swiftly, the sweat dripping from his face in great pearls, he carried out the same routine with the pins, while the other two packed plastic explosive into the yawning steel breeches. Red took the time pencil from between his teeth and was about to poke it into the evil-smelling brown mass when Hardt shouted, 'No time for that now!' He pulled out a grenade and ripped off the pin, keeping his finger, however, over the catch. 'All right, you guys,' he yelled to the others, 'move back now … come on!'

'Fall back, rally on the CO!' van Fleet commanded.

Slowly, firing as they moved back — and Hardt could tell from the hollow screams coming from the unseen enemy that their bullets were finding their mark — they came up the corridor, while their CO searched wildly for some way out of the trap they found themselves in. Suddenly he spotted it. A small metal door let in the wall at the end of the tunnel and equipped with steel handles, rather like the watertight doors he remembered from the troopship which had taken him to North Africa in 1942. 'Red, Limey,' he yelled above the racket of the fight, 'up the corridor to that door — cover me and the other guys as they fall back!' He raised his voice. 'Van Fleet!'

The bespectacled Executive Officer swung round. 'Skipper?'

'Pull out — up the tunnel to that door!'

'Roger, skipper!'

Firing, stopping, moving again like the trained veterans they were, the handful of T-Force kept the élite German officer cadets, still not visible to a tensely waiting Hardt, at bay.

Wheels passed his CO bleeding from a graze on his forehead. 'Jesus, Major,' he gasped as he did so, 'what wouldn't I give to be behind the wheel of Old Baldy now!'

Triggerman followed him, his whole attention concentrated on the enemy, as he fired short precise bursts down the tunnel, so cool even at this moment of high tension that he was not wasting his ammunition unnecessarily.

Van Fleet came level with Hardt, the barrel of his grease gun already glowing a dull red. The first German poked his head cautiously around the corner, but not cautiously enough. Van

Fleet fired without seeming to take aim. The German reeled back screaming, his face shattered. Van Fleet laughed.

Behind him Hardt heard Red throw open the door with a great hollow boom. It was now or never. 'Van Fleet,' he yelled, 'when I throw this grenade, run like hell for that door. Got it?'

'Got it!'

'Okay — *NOW!*' In that same instant Hardt lobbed the grenade neatly into the wide open breech of the nearest gun and began tearing down the corridor, German bullets stitching a pattern of blue sparks at his heels, as if the devil himself were after him.

He crashed through the door, followed a second later by van Fleet.

A cry of triumph rose from the ranks of the Germans massing at the corner. '*Los*' an officer shouted at the same moment that the plastic explosive went up. The great detonation, followed an instant later by a second one, tore the heart out of the first and then the second gun, sending fist-sized, red-hot lumps of steel scything through the packed Germans. Men went down screaming crazily everywhere, limbs flailing wildly, as a chilling wind howled down the corridor and slammed the door shut behind the last of the Americans with a sound of hollow finality.

CHAPTER 4

'It kinds looks as if the Krauts have got us by the short and curlies, skipper,' van Fleet said quietly, as the sound of the second pair of explosions died away.

'What's the matter, Lieutenant?' Triggerman guarding the door sneered, his grease gun at the ready. 'You turning chicken on us?'

'Knock it off, Trigger,' Hardt commanded routinely, his mind racing wildly, as he sized up the little room and tried to figure out some way of escape for his trapped men.

It seemed to be some kind of tool shed for the guns. Around the walls there were the great spanners used for releasing the guns' recoil springs, replacement ramrod tops, metal barrels filled with oil to fill the breech system. But it wasn't the tools which interested a frantic Hardt at that moment. It was the long angled slit in the place's far wall, which he guessed allowed air to circulate in the room but did not allow any light to escape to the outside.

Limey, always quicker off the mark than the rest of Old Baldy's crew, caught his look and said, 'I've already had a shufti, sir, while you was at the door.'

'And?' Hardt demanded.

'It's the outer wall, sir. That's for sure.'

'Then we could squeeze through and get out that way,' Dutchie exclaimed in sudden delight.

'Natch,' Limey replied easily, 'that is unless yer wanted to break yer stupid Yankee head. We only happen to be', he shrugged quickly, 'perhaps thirty or forty feet above the sodding ground, that's all.'

Dutchie's look of hope vanished as swiftly as it had come. 'I was just thinking.'

'Well, yer know what thought did, don't you mate,' Limey responded. 'He shat hissen!'

Hardt ignored the exchange. Swiftly he pushed by Limey and thrust his upper body into the angled slit. By twisting his head at an awkward angle, he could just make out the ground below, illuminated by the glare of the dying XX Corps barrage. Limey was right. Even if they could get out of the chamber they found themselves in without being shot, they stood a good chance of breaking their necks at that height.

He straightened up again just in time to hear the first frightening hiss of the tool the Germans had brought up to winkle them out and see the inside of the door glow a dull-red.

'*Oxy-acetylene torch*!' Wheels cursed swiftly. 'The bastards'll burn a hole in the door and blast the hell out of us at their goddam leisure!'

Even Triggerman's usual truculent sneer vanished. 'What did you say, Wheels?' he asked, backing away a little as the glow started to spread, slowly, but inevitably.

'You heard, Triggerman!' Wheels snapped, following his example.

Eventually all of them were hugging the far wall, listening to the subdued hum of many voices on the other side of the door and the steady hiss of the torch, which seemed a tangible symbol of what was going to happen to them soon.

Hastily Hardt pulled himself together. 'Okay, guys,' he shouted, though there was no need for him to raise his voice with the men crowded all around him at touching distance. 'There's only one way out — through that hole. We'll just have to chance our arm. If we break something', he left the sentence unfinished as the hiss of the torch died away, leaving behind it a sudden stillness, a silence which was more menacing than all the noise and mayhem which had gone before it.

'But sir, there's a rope — *here*,' It was Dutchie, his finger pointing dramatically at something stacked neatly in front of his big feet, 'Well, I guess it's a kind of a rope.'

Hardt spun round as did the others, their blood-shot eyes suddenly filled with hope. Dutchie was pointing at a heap of thick steel hawser. Big Red, who had once been in the artillery before the war, recognised it first. 'It's for hauling back the breech spring when they're testing it, sir,' he explained.

'How long do you think it could be?' Hardt asked urgently.

'Could be anything up to twenty or thirty feet, sir, depending upon what calibre cannon it's intended for.'

Hardt breathed out hard. 'It might just do it,' he said hastily. 'Okay, break it out, fellers — and make it snappy!'

Behind them at the door came the first reverberating clang of a sledgehammer. The Krauts were trying to beat out the circle of metal burnt free by the oxy-acetylene torch. The hollow boom lent speed to their hands. Fumbling frantically they unfurled the stiff, unwieldy hawser, hooked at one end so that it could grasp the buffer spring of the cannon it was being used to service.

'Quick, Limey,' Hardt snapped, 'into that slit and take the end of it with you.'

Hastily Limey, the smallest of the T-Force men, crawled into the angled hole, while Red searched desperately for somewhere to fasten the hooked end.

'All right, I'm ready, sir,' Limey's voice came from within the hole, just as Red slotted one of the giant spanners through the hook and wedged it sideways across the aperture.

'Okay, Limey,' Hardt yelled, 'let the rope down. We've got it anchored here.'

'Geronimo!' Limey yelled, using the war cry of the para-troops, and let the rope go down the wall. 'Say goodbye to everybody for me!' His voice stopped suddenly, as he disappeared over the side.

Swiftly Triggerman and Wheels followed him, while van Fleet and Hardt faced the door, weapons at the ready, prepared to shoot the first face to appear at the hole. Now it was Big Red's turn. Aided by Dutchie Schulze, he fitted his big body awkwardly into the slot, grunting hard with the effort.

'For Chrissake, Sarge, get ya ass in,' Dutchie pleaded desperately, 'or the Krauts are gonna blow a hole in it... *Move it!*'

'I am moving it, you stupid bastard!' Big Red yelled, as he wriggled frantically, trying to slide his bulk through the hole.

Under other circumstances the scene would have been highly funny, but not now. The circle of metal was beginning to give and the Germans outside were stepping up their hammering, urged on by the triumphant voice of an officer. Hardt raised his carbine and shouted angrily, 'Dutchie, kick his fat butt through, willya, for God's sake!'

'He's done it, sir,' Dutchie answered swiftly, 'I'm going now, if you don't need me?'

'No. *Quick!* —'

Abruptly the metal gave. It clattered alarmingly to the floor in front of the two officers. Hardt caught a glimpse of a white face and fired. There was a scream of sheer agony and the face, now mangled and bloody, disappeared.

'*Los, Leute!*' the officer's voice outside yelled. '*Her mit dem Flammenwerfer!... Schnell!*'

'*Flammenwerfer* — flame thrower!' A thrill of fear shot through Hardt's body. In a moment of total recall, he remembered that terrible confrontation with the Kraut armed with a flame-thrower, who had mutilated him for life. For an instant he couldn't control the violent trembling of his hand. Then he pulled himself together. 'Van Fleet,' he croaked, hardly recognising his own voice, 'get through that hole. *Quick*! they're bringing up a flame-thrower!'

Van Fleet dived to the hole. Outside there was a sudden soft hiss. Hardt recognised it immediately. They had ignited the flame-thrower. Next moment the German officer's voice ordered: 'Poke it through the hole, man! Burn 'em out like rats, quick!'

Blindly, his face contorted with terror, Hardt fired a volley of wild shots through the hole, while van Fleet slid into the opening, and he kept firing until all of a sudden the carbine died in his hands. He had exhausted the magazine! He let it drop to the floor with a clatter. Seized by absolute, uncontrollable panic, he ran for the hole, just as that terrible nozzle began to poke its way through the door.

'Pull the trigger, you craphead!' an angry voice ordered outside.

Desperately Hardt squirmed into the dark hole. Behind him the room he had just left glowed a terrifying blood-red. A tremendous heat seared his back. He yelped with pain and struggled on, his Ike jacket hanging from him in scorched, burnt rags. Madly he clawed his way to the opening. Down below he could just make out the ground. With frantic hands, he grabbed the metal hawser, sobbing for breath.

Just as the room behind glowed again and that terrible, all-consuming flame shot down the aperture, he flung himself over the side, ignoring the cruel tearing of the wire at his hands and began to scramble wildly down it.

Hardt lay slumped on the muddy ground, completely exhausted, staring blindly, apparently unable to move, although he knew he had to make a decision at once. The roar of the XX Corps' covering barrage had died away to be replaced by the chatter of the BAR team guarding the entrance to the battery. Obviously the men inside were trying to break out and it wouldn't be long before the German troops down below in the city would start coming up the hill to their aid.

'Skipper,' van Fleet said urgently, 'what's the deal? Do we try to have a crack at the other two turrets?'

Hardt shook his head violently, like a very tired man trying to shake himself awake. 'No, too late for that,' he replied, his voice regaining its old strength and decision as he spoke. 'The whole goddam place is alerted now. We've done our best. Let's get the hell outa here while the going's still good.'

'You can say that again, Major,' Limey agreed. 'If we don't move out soon, we'll be right up the sodding creek without a sodding paddle!'

Hardt staggered to his feet. He fumbled with his whistle and put it to his bone dry lips. As best he could, he blew three shrill blasts on it: the signal he had agreed upon with his men at the briefing.

All around, the T-Force GIs started to rise from their foxholes and move slowly down the hill in little groups of five and six, heading for their hiding place in the shed. Hardt turned to his waiting crew. 'Okay, we're gonna move out too in a minute. Triggerman, Wheels and Dutchie, keep your eyes on that slit up there. If anybody pokes his head through, let him have it!'

'With the greatest of pleasure,' Triggerman snarled.

'Okay, you three, start moving back — slowly.' He turned to the others. 'Red, Clarry and Limey, come with me. We've got to help that BAR team to get out. Okay, let's go!'

Awkwardly they stumbled across the rough, pitted ground in the darkness, guided a little by the muzzle flash of the Browning automatic rifle posted at the door and the crazy zig-zag of the German tracer from within.

'Right, Red,' Hardt ordered, 'bail 'em out, while we keep you covered.'

'Roger, sir!'

Head ducked down between his big shoulders, the massive NCO hurtled towards the entrance like some professional football player on an end run. A dozen feet from the gate, he dived forward under the hail of tracer coming from within and slid through the wet grass to the sweating GIs crouching around the chattering machine gun. He snapped something to them. Then, standing upright, completely contemptuous of the enemy fire, his legs spread apart like a cowboy in a Hollywood movie shoot-out, he started pouring a hail of fire into the fort, while the BAR crew moved back.

Hardt cupped his hands round his mouth. 'Red,' he yelled frantically, come on, you silly big bastard, move back now, while we cover you!'

He saw the big NCO's back stiffen. For a moment it looked as if he might ignore the order, for now his temper, as fiery-red as his hair, was aroused. But he lowered his grease gun, turned and began doubling back the way he had come. From within the entrance, there was a bellow of rage. 'Here they come,' Hardt cried.

The other two tensed expectantly. Next instant the officer-cadets, as brave as they were stupid, poured out of the fort to be met by the concentrated fire of the BAR and the grease guns. It wasn't war, just sheer massacre. Limbs flailing, they fell on all sides, blocking the entrance with their twitching bodies.

'Come on,' Hardt cried hurriedly, 'let's go now!'

In the sudden silence, that seemed somehow louder and more oppressive than all the frightening clamour that had gone before, the last of the T-Force men began to stumble down the steep slope after their comrades...

CHAPTER 5

'Well, whore,' Commissar Gallo of the underground *Franc-Tireurs et Partisans* demanded, looking up at Wanda, standing there in the candle-lit cellar looking pale and not a little frightened at what she was now doing, what does your kind want from us?'

'Can I sit down?' she quavered, 'the bombardment and the way here ... my legs —'

'All right, woman,' the skinny Communist Maquis man with the evil face interrupted her brutally. 'Jo,' he rapped to the leather-jacketed sentry guarding the cellar door, 'give the woman a box!'

Jo, a giant with the squashed nose and thickened cheeks of the boxer he had once been, pushed a box over to the shaking woman contemptuously, 'Park your fat ass on that,' he ordered thickly.

Wanda sat down gratefully and stared at the dapper man facing her with his thin, cruel, bloodless lips and his empty, frightening eyes. This was the first time she had met Commissar Gallo, who controlled Metz's Communist Underground. But she knew of him and what she had heard was bad, very bad. Recruiting his Maquis from the steel and iron workers of the suburbs, he had strengthened the force by a sizeable strong-arm squad of pimps and petty crooks from the old city's underworld. In 1942 when Germany was still winning in Russia, and there were many in Metz who actively supported or at least tolerated the Boche, he had kidnapped a squad of young German recruits on a night march from Metz to Mars-le-Tour. After sending appropriate notes to the

German controlled newspapers and the German Commandant he had emasculated the teenaged recruits. The result had been as Gallo had expected. The Germans had rounded up a hundred young Frenchmen, shot one in ten of them and sent the rest to their concentration camps. Thereafter there were fewer civilians in Metz who supported the Boche. One year later his strong-arm squad had broken into the German hospital near the University and had raped six German Red Cross nurses in front of their helpless patients. Again there had been a sensation in the garrison city and the Germans had carried out large-scale raids in reprisal. By mid-1944, with the Boche losing everywhere, Gallo and his Communist partisans had become a real power in the city. When the Gaullist Maquis had slipped out of Metz as the Americans surrounded it, he had remained behind, determined to be first on the scene when the city was liberated, ready at once to seize control.

This was the man to whom Wanda was now entrusting her fate. But she knew there was no other way. Harzig, the fat Fritz, had bungled things so often in the past that she no longer trusted him to get her back to her native Provence safely. She would bargain her own way out without him.

'Comrade Gallo,' she began hesitantly, no longer the masterful woman she was during her working hours.

'*Comrade* Gallo,' the little Commisar laughed and ran his hand over his black, wetly-gleaming hair, 'Did you hear that, Jo? The bourgeois *horizontale* calls us comrade now?'

Jo laughed gruffly.

Wanda pressed on with her explanation desperately, comforted a little by the feel of her case with its precious contents at the side of her plump leg. 'So you see, the Fritzes are going to use the Americans to get them out and into his headquarters,' she concluded, noting the look of interest in

Gallo s eyes with a certain feeling of satisfaction. 'But of course, as soon as I found out from my Fritz, the Gestapo man, I knew I had to stop their plan. That's why I came to you as soon as I found out where you might be located. For the cause, for victory...' She let the words peter out lamely.

Gallo smiled cynically. 'Yes,' he echoed, 'for the cause, for victory.' His smile vanished. 'How do you know that the Boche will be able to take the Americans?' he asked.

'Because they will be waiting for them at the place they are using to hide.'

'And that is?'

She told him and he made a quick note on the back of an envelope. For what seemed a long time, he stared down at the scribble thoughtfully, while she waited expectantly.

Eugene Gallo had always had an eye for the main chance ever since he had joined the 'Party of the Future' during the days of the Popular Front and realised that in its ranks he would never have to do another day's work in the black misery of the Lorraine pits ever again. Now he realised that if he helped the Americans, it well might give him the edge in the struggle with the Gaullists which would certainly ensue as soon as the city was liberated.

Finally he became aware of the woman's presence again. 'And you, whore, what do you want? Why have you brought me this information, eh?'

Wanda Lejeune jumped at the opportunity offered her. 'Get your people to guide me through the lines and let me get away from this terrible place, Monsieur Gallo,' she answered quickly. 'That's all I ask from you for the information.'

Gallo laughed, but there was no warmth of humour in the sound. 'Is that all? You want me to risk the lives of my comrades to get a Boche whore like you through the front.

Four years on your back for the Fritzes and now you think you can get out of it as easily as that.' He wagged his forefinger in front of her face suddenly. 'No, no, my little Boche cabbage, you're not going to have it that good.'

'But Monsieur Gallo,' she began.

The Communist leader ignored her pleas. 'Jo, toss her to the boys. They've been pretty horny of late. Let them poke her hole — if they want to — and you'd better see what she's got in that case she's keeping at her legs so carefully.'

Jo grinned slowly. 'With pleasure, Comrade Gallo,' he growled and advanced on Wanda.

'No, no,' she cried desperately and grabbed the case's handle. Jo did not even hesitate. He grabbed her hand. He grunted. Effortlessly he bent her fingers back and she screamed piteously as he broke her fingers — one by one. Without giving her a second look as she crumpled back on the box, sobbing with pain, her face the colour of clay, he opened the case to reveal the silver. 'Not bad, Comrade,' he chortled, 'this lot'll buy the boys a lot of booze, eh?'

Gallo was no longer listening, however. His mind was full of the new problem the whore had presented him with. How was he going to solve it?

It was the same problem that faced an ashen-faced Major Hardt at that very moment, as he raised his hands in the air, realising that the SS men in their camouflaged smocks meant business. There was no alternative. Like the rest of the T-Force, he and the rearguard had walked straight into the trap the Krauts had set for them in the abandoned workshop.

As the fat civilian in the long, creaking leather coat, who seemed to be in charge of the troops, thrust his pistol back in his pocket, Hardt felt a sense of guilt, of utter helpless inadequacy, settle down on his shoulders like a heavy weight. They had come so far and done so well — to be pipped at the post.

The fat civilian caught the look on his face and smiled in cruel triumph. 'You are very happy, Major, yes?' he said in stilted, heavily accented English.

Hardt did not answer his question.

Without the slightest hesitation, Harzig brought back his fist and smashed it straight into Hardt's face.

The Major reeled back against the wall, blood spurting from his nose. Big Red dashed forward. But a swift blow with a rifle butt in his stomach from one of the SS men doubled him up before he had got even within striking distance of the grinning Gestapo man. He sank to the dirty floor groaning softly through gritted teeth.

'You see, Major,' Harzig said softly, 'you must not be arrogant with me, yes?' He smiled again, showing his gold teeth.

'Yes,' Hardt replied, wiping away the blood where the cheap metal ring on Harzig's middle finger had split his nose.

'Good, then now we understand ourselves.' Harzig came closer and Hardt could smell the stench of his cigar and garlic laden breath. 'And before we are done, we are understanding ourselves even better.'

'What do you mean?' Hardt asked carefully, knowing that in spite of his comic English this elderly civilian was dangerous, very dangerous.

'I mean this,' Harzig's smile vanished suddenly. 'You, *mein Lieber Major*, are to help us to kill that cowboy General of yours in Nancy.'

'*What?*'

'Yes, to kill your famous General Patton…'

PART FOUR: OPERATION CUCKOO

'We are in other words a punishment unit of the SS — the
Ascension Day Commando, as we call ourselves. In English
you might say a suicide squad. To be brief then, we have
nothing to lose and everything to gain.'

Sturmbannführer Krass to Major Hardt

CHAPTER 1

Sturmbannführer Krass of the Hitler Youth Division, his young arrogant face puckered up by a bayonet wound that bisected his right cheek from eyebrow to chin, looked with bottomless contempt at the two dishevelled American officers whom the Gestapo man had paraded in front of him. 'Are these they?' he demanded coldly in his too perfect English.

'Yes, *Sturmbannführer*,' Harzig stuttered, not knowing how to translate the SS rank.

'Call me, Captain, man,' Krauss rapped, not taking his hard gaze off the two prisoners. 'Your names are Hardt and van Fleet and you belong to the Third Army's T-Force?'

'Name, number and rank,' van Fleet said wearily. 'You know the Convention? We don't have to say any more.'

Krass looked at the Lieutenant as if he had just crawled out of the woodwork. 'The Armed SS has long torn up that piece of humbug,' he snapped. 'Besides what Convention can protect people like you? You are caught behind our lines in our uniform. You are unpersons. You have no rights. Understand that!' His voice was glacial with menace.

Van Fleet's gaze sank to the floor. He understood well enough. They were already as good as dead and it was only by an effort of will that he kept himself from screaming out in naked fear.

For a moment there was no sound in the room, save the creak of Harzig's absurd leather coat every time he breathed, then Krass said: 'Let me first explain something about myself and my men. We are from every division of the Armed SS. I, myself, was in the Hitler Youth, as you can see from my arm

patch, before I was posted to this unit as punishment for a —'
the bemedalled SS officer hesitated only a fraction of a second
— 'certain misdemeanour, which I need not go into here.' Out
of the corner of his eye, Krass caught the look on the fat cop's
face and realised he knew about that wretched business with
the Russian boy. If it had not been for his Knight's Cross and
Himmler's Personal intervention he would now be wearing the
purple badge of the homosexual in some concentration camp
or other — and the whole thing had been so perfectly
harmless! Hurriedly he dismissed the episode from his mind.
'We are in other words a punishment unit of the SS — the
Ascension Day Commando as we call ourselves. In English
you might say a suicide squad. To be brief then, we have
nothing to lose and everything to gain.'

'Why are you telling us all this?' Hardt asked, speaking for
the first time since they had been separated from the men that
morning and brought to General Priess's Headquarters. 'What
has all this got to do with us?' he added with a sudden burst of
anger.

'Because, Major, just as you are as good as dead, we are too
until we have proved ourselves fit to be accepted back in our
original units. And', he raised his well-manicured finger in
warning, 'we are capable of doing anything to achieve that aim.
Make no mistake of that. Now, General Priess has selected me
and a group of my men to carry out the assassination of
General Patton, which we will carry out with your assistance.'

Hardt looked at the SS officer in open-mouthed, undisguised
amazement: the German had uttered the words, as if they were
a simple statement of fact, completely devoid of any doubt.
'What the Sam Hill do you mean,' he stuttered, '*with our
assistance?*'

'You and your men will leave the city the way you came —
Maizières, wasn't it?' he asked Harzig.

Harzig nodded.

'When you reach your own lines, you will state you are going
to proceed to the Third Army Commander's HQ at Nancy to
report to the Commanding General personally. No one will
attempt to stop you — after all you are Patton's personal
reconnaissance force. It will be the logical thing for you to do.'

'But —'

The young SS officer did not seem to hear his objection. He
carried on in the same cold, confident manner as before.
'Naturally the two armoured cars and the half-track you
abandoned at the locomotive shed at Maizières will contain my
men and I personally will be with you in the first jeep —'

'*But you must be off your goddam head!*' Hardt finally managed to
get the words out. 'Do you really think we are going to help
you to kill our own Commanding General, man? Hellfire man,
you must be nuts!'

'I don't think so, Major,' Krass replied, completely unmoved
by the American's passionate outburst. He pressed the button
on the desk in front of him. The door was opened immediately
by the one-eyed brute of an NCO, with the arm patch of the
Adolf Hitler Bodyguard, who had escorted them to the HQ.
'*Sturmbannführer?*' he barked at the top of his voice.

'Held, deal with the first three of them.'

'*Jawohl, Sturmbannführer.*'

The NCO disappeared, leaving the four of them sunk in a
silence, which was finally disturbed by the harsh ring of heavy
jackboots on the cobbles of the courtyard below. Krass
crooked a finger at the two American officers. 'Come over
here a moment, please,' he ordered.

Reluctantly van Fleet and Hardt crossed to the window, which looked out on to the gloomy, walled courtyard. Down below a file of SS men, armed with rifles, were drawn up at the position of attention, facing three of the young replacements who had joined T-Force at Verdun. Their hands were tied behind their backs so tightly that their chests were thrust out as if they were challenging the squad of hard-faced SS men. But Hardt knew that his young men were feeling anything but brave at this particular moment. He swallowed hard, already sick to his heart with the knowledge of what must now inevitably happen, and asked thickly, 'What are you going to do with them?'

'Isn't it obvious?' Krass replied almost casually. He took out a long black ivory cigarette holder and placed a cigarette in it with deliberate ceremony, while the one-eyed NCO took up his position at the side of the file.

'*Achtung!*' the NCO cried. '*Legt an!*' Like automatons the squad of SS men raised their rifles and pointed them at the three young prisoners.

'But you can't do this!' van Fleet screamed, his face contorted wildly. 'You simply can't shoot them in cold —'

'*Feuer!*' the rest of his words were drowned by the hoarse command and the crash of the rifles. The replacements shuddered violently. One screamed in agony, but the other two went down without a sound. The one-eyed NCO slipped open his pistol holster and drew out his Walter. Slowly and deliberately, as if he had done this sort of thing often enough before, he walked over and examined the first man crumpled on the blood-stained cobbles. He straightened up again and examined the next one. He was obviously dead too, for he moved on without making use of his pistol. He touched the shoulder of the one who had screamed. The young soldier shuddered violently and his head rolled from one side to the other, as he moaned in mortal agony. The NCO placed one big hand on the side of his pain-twisted young face and held him firmly in position thus, while he poked the muzzle of his pistol at the dying man's skull. He took a quick breath and pressed the trigger. The American's skull shattered. The NCO looked at his suddenly blood-spattered hand in disgust.

'Well?' Krass inquired coldly, his voice completely without emotion. 'In exactly five minutes, *Rottenführer* Held has orders to bring out another three of your men and shoot them. And he will continue to shoot them at regular intervals until you agree to my plan or', he shrugged slightly in the continental fashion, 'T-Force exists no more.' He looked at Hardt directly and took a deep draw at his cigarette holder.

Hardt felt the bitter grey wave of defeat sweep through his body. His mouth was filled with a sour taste. The scar-faced SS officer was absolutely capable of carrying out his threat, he knew that. He, Hardt, would have to agree or see his beloved T-Force destroyed in the courtyard below, where the three corpses were already beginning to stiffen in the raw morning air. But if he did agree, he was risking the life of America's most aggressive General, the one man who might make the difference between victory and defeat in Germany in the months to come. Hardt bit his bottom lip hard, while the young SS officer and the gross Gestapo man watched him curiously. What was he going to do? *What?*

'Skipper, don't do it,' van Fleet broke into his reverie. 'They're fooling. Even they daren't shoot over a hundred of our guys in cold blood —'

But the harsh crunch of the NCO's boots below accompanied by the softer shuffle of American combat boots, as he fetched three more victims from the cells, gave the lie to the words, and they died on his lips.

For one brief, heart-sickening moment, Hardt almost gave up, unable to accept the responsibility one way or another. Then he pulled himself together swiftly, banishing his indecision as a form of self-indulgence which was costing men's lives. Hope was gone, but not totally. As long as he and his men were alive, there was still a chance, however faint, that they might be able to reverse the situation.

As the one-eyed NCO barked his first order and the firing squad snapped to attention, Hardt licked his dry lips and said faintly, 'All right, you win.'

'I always do,' *Sturmbannführer* Krass said softly and took another draw at his holder.

CHAPTER 2

Gallo and Jo were waiting for Harzig when he opened the door to Wanda's room. Before he could cry out in surprise at the presence of the two strangers, Jo kneed him neatly and professionally, sending him reeling back against the dirty wallpaper, vomiting his upper plate from his mouth. A moment later Gallo had locked the door and pushed him, still clutching his injured crotch, on to the ancient brass bed.

Gallo gave him a minute to recover, then snapped, 'All right, you Boche pig, stop that rubbish! I've got some questions to ask you.' When the Gestapo man did not respond, he nodded to Jo.

With the palm of his dirty hand he rammed Harzig's upper plate back into his wide open mouth and an instant later slapped him quickly back and forth across the face in the French fashion, grunting between slaps, 'Didn't you … hear … what the Chief … said, prick?'

'Yes, yes,' Harzig blubbered, 'I heard… But please, please stop!'

'Now?' Jo queried Gallo without stopping the beating.

Gallo inclined his head.

Jo stopped, and stepped aside to let Gallo get closer to the sobbing, crimson-faced German. 'Listen you Fritz sack of excrement, my name is Gallo. I have slit the gizzards of more Fritzes than you've had hot dinners. And I'll slit yours too if you don't answer my questions — *immediately*. Do you understand?'

Harzig, who knew of the Communist Commissar's terrible reputation in Metz, nodded, the tears hurrying down his flushed cheeks, not trusting himself to speak.

'Good. Now then, I know most of what you're up to already. From your fat whore Wanda. So it's no use trying to lie to me. But I don't know the route you people are going to take with those captured *Amis* and where you're going to kill the American General — Patton or whatever his name is.' He paused momentarily. 'All right, Fritz, let's have it?'

Harzig continued to blubber, his head hanging down on his chest so that the two French bastards could not see the look in his eyes, his mind racing wildly as he considered his position. If he told them what he knew he would never get out of Metz, but if he didn't, would they dare kill him? Gallo's reputation was fearsome, he knew that. But he also knew that he would never risk his own neck — he left that to his subordinates, those dumb steelworkers and miners of his who had imbibed Communism with their mother's milk. Besides, there were regular German patrols through the red light district on the look-out for absentees and deserters from the front. Surely Gallo would not dare carry out his threat under those circumstances!

'Well?' Gallo demanded threateningly. 'Have you gone to sleep, you German prick? I asked you a question. What's your answer, *sale con?*'

Harzig did not raise his head and kept his mouth shut.

Gallo nodded to Jo. The big ex-boxer reached out one massive hand and grabbed Harzig by his thinning hair. He pulled hard. With a yelp of acute agony, Harzig shot his head up. 'The chief asked you a question,' Jo grunted.

'I don't know… Honestly, I don't,' Harzig cried through gritted teeth, his eyes squeezed to slits of pain. 'Please … believe me!'

'Crap!' Gallo rapped contemptuously. 'You know all right, you fat turd. It was your plan all along. They will have told you all. Don't try to shit me.'

But Harzig, his mind made up, knowing that his very life depended upon his remaining silent, kept his mouth obstinately closed, while Gallo glowered at him. Suddenly he spoke. 'I hear that you are fond of Wanda's special treatments. They give you pleasure, you pervert, don't they? Well, perhaps if you are given a little pleasure, you might be more receptive to our questions, *hein*?'

Harzig shuddered, but the shudder was totally unlike those delicious ones that Wanda's threats had once induced in him. The man facing him would not hesitate to flog him to death in order to obtain the information he sought. 'But they'll hear the screams I make outside!' he objected desperately, trying to save himself from the terrible beating to come.

'So what, *ordure*!' Gallo answered easily. 'Are screams anything unusual from this place? That is what you perverts pay your money for, isn't it?' He walked over to Wanda's cupboard. He stood there apparently in deep thought, taking his time about selecting the instrument of punishment he wanted. But finally he chose an ox-gut whip with a flexible steel rod inside it. With a cold smile on his thin pale face he swished it menacingly through the air.

Harzig shivered violently. He knew it well. He had asked Wanda to use it on him one time only. But it had sufficed. The lash had cut to the very bone.

'*Tu as compris, salaud?*' Gallo said softly. 'I'll whip you to death if you don't tell me what I want to know.'

Harzig bit his bottom lip hard to prevent himself from losing control altogether. Gallo meant every word. But somehow he must play for time till one of the patrols came down the street; then he would scream for help. *Time … time*, that was what he needed.

Abruptly Gallo ordered, 'Take the fat pig's shirt off.'

Harzig tried to struggle, but he was like a puny child in Jo's mighty grasp. With one grunt, he ripped Harzig s shirt down, revealing his unhealthily white body. A moment later he had pinioned the Gestapo man's hands behind his back, and tied them together with the remnants of his shirt. Another grunt and his big paw pushed Harzig's face forward on the bed.

'All right, *crapule*, now taste this!' Gallo cried and brought the cruel lash down.

Harzig screamed piteously as the whip struck his back, cutting deep into the flabby flesh. His spine arched like a bow and suddenly his whole body seemed on fire.

'Well, what is their route?' Gallo demanded, breathing hard.

'I don't know… Honestly, I don't —'

His words ended in another scream as Gallo brought the ox-gut whip down once more. And again! And again, while Harzig writhed furiously, shrieking, high and hysterical, like a woman. But Gallo had no mercy. His face lathered with sweat, his eyes filled with a sudden feverish excitement at the side of the fat Boche's wriggling body, the white flesh streaked over and over again with bloody stripes, he beat Harzig mercilessly in a fashion that had even Jo gaping at his chief in amazement. But still Harzig refused to talk. Finally Gallo, his chest heaving as if he had just run a race, had to stop. Letting his tired arm drop, he wiped the beads of sweat from his brow and gasped, 'All right, Jo, you take over. I'm buggered!'

Before Jo could take up the whip, however, there was the sound of heavy nailed boots on the cobbles outside. '*Streife!*' a harsh German voice commanded. '*Ausweise und Pässe bereithalten!*' Harzig tried to raise his head. Hastily Jo pressed his mouth into the bloodied covers, and flashed Gallo a look of alarm.

Gallo reacted swiftly. 'Gag him, Jo! And wait here, I'll be back!' He sped out of the door. Below, the patrol was banging on the doors and there were shrieking girls and cursing soldiers everywhere. He ran into the next room. A skinny woman, naked to the waist, was struggling into a kimono, while a soldier on the bed, completely naked save for his boots and helmet was cursing drunkenly at being disturbed at the height of his passion. Gallo ignored him. 'You,' he rapped and grasped the girl by her thin wrist, 'I need you!'

'Are you crazy?' she retorted. 'What the hell do you think —'

'My name's Gallo,' he hissed threateningly. 'If you don't want that whore's mug of yours to undergo a little surgery, cabbage, you'd better come quick!'

The whore made no further protest. Leaving the drunken soldier still cursing on the rumpled bed, she followed Gallo into the other room where Harzig lay gagged, his little pig-like eyes almost popping out with fury. 'Here,' Gallo thrust the whip into her hand, 'when the Boche come in, start knocking hell out of him — and for Chrissake, take that blouse off so that they can get a load of your tits. All right, Jo, into that cupboard. Leave this to me!'

A few minutes later a solid MP with a broad, humorous face stalked into the room, rifle slung over his shoulder, hands dug deep into the pockets of his greatcoat. 'Hello, hello,' he boomed as he took in the little scene being performed in front of him, 'what have we here, eh?'

The whore dropped the bloody whip and turned around, as if surprised. The MP touched one hand to his helmet, as if in salute and grunted, 'Nice pair of lungs you've got on yer there, M'selle. But yer might catch pneumonia if yer not careful.' He laughed thickly at his own humour and the blank look on the whore's face. 'And you, Frog,' he turned suspiciously on Gallo, 'what are you doing here?'

Gallo gave him a little humble bow. 'I am a friend of the lady,' he explained in his fair German. 'The gentleman of the Gestapo says it gives him greater pleasure when I watch.' He shrugged. 'A little quirk of his, M'sieu, you understand?'

The big MP whistled through his front teeth. 'Gestapo eh?' he exclaimed. 'What next!'

'His pass is here, sir,' Gallo indicated Harzig's jacket lying over the chair.

The MP shook his head. 'Nix, I want nothing to do with those laddos.' He bent his mouth closer to Gallo and the Communist leader caught a whiff of schnaps-charged breath. 'But tell the whore to give his fat Gestapo arse a couple of biffs from me, will you, Frog.' He winked.

Gallo winked back conspiratorially. 'I'll tell her expressly, sir, when you have gone.'

The MP touched his hand to his helmet casually. 'It's going to be a hot time in the old town tonight, ain't it,' he commented and strolled out.

Five minutes later Harzig was singing like a little bird, his last chance gone now. 'They will leave the Metz area by Maizières,' he gasped, wiping the tears from his trembling cheeks. 'Then they'll swing round Metz behind the *Ami* lines...' His statement was interrupted by a great sob.

'Get on with it, pig!' Gallo called threateningly.

'They'll head south for Nancy.'

'Why Nancy?'

'Because it's that American General's headquarters,' Harzig quavered.

'And where are they going to try to kill him?'

'Captain Krass —'

'Who's he?' Gallo asked swiftly.

'The head of the Ascension Day Commando, who will carry out the assassination.'

'Go on.'

'Well, he says it would be too risky to try to kill him at his headquarters. Too many witnesses. Instead they are going to do it at his private quarters. There they'll only have his staff and perhaps a couple of MPs to contend with. Captain Krass thinks they'll be able to do it and get away before the *Amis* wake up to what has happened.'

'A brave man or a complete fool, your Captain Krass,' Gallo commented slowly, absorbing the information. Then he was businesslike again. He nodded to Jo, and then at the bleeding man on the bed. Harzig's crimson face blanched. 'What are you going to do?'

Instead of replying, Jo picked up Harzig's jacket, removed the wallet and put it in his own pocket; then he drew his Luger and wrapped the jacket around the pistol.

Suddenly Harzig realised what was going to happen. He slid from the bed and dropped to his knees, his hands held up in the classic plea for mercy. '*Bitte, bitte, nicht schiessen,*' he called fervently, his French forgotten now, '*nicht schiessen!*'

He broke off suddenly, as Jo thrust the muffled pistol to his temple. '*NEIN!*' he screamed, '*NEIN, NICHT DAS —*'

Jo pulled the trigger. The fat Gestapo man was lifted clean from his knees and flung against the opposite wall, the top of his head gone. His false teeth bulging absurdly from between his lips, Harzig's lifeless body began to slide down the wall, a blood-red smear trailing behind it...

CHAPTER 3

The little convoy set off from Maizières Station just before dawn. To the front and rear a Staghound, filled with Krass's vicious-looking SS killers, kept watch on the sullen T-Force men, while each of their jeeps had an SS criminal in GI uniform guarding the unarmed prisoners. Krass himself, immaculate in his US Captain's uniform, rode in Old Baldy just behind the lead Staghound. He sat to the rear of the half-track, pistol at the ready, his eyes fixed suspiciously on the crew.

Slowly the line of vehicles picked their way down the track through the minefield, grinding along in first gear, coming ever closer to the line held by the survivors of the dead Captain's black soldiers. Sitting next to Wheels, who was driving, Hardt's brain raced as he tried to figure out some way to turn the tables on the scar-faced SS Captain. But Krass had seemingly thought of every eventuality. Although the T-Force men still had their weapons — without them they would have aroused suspicion in the American lines — they were unloaded; and as Krass had warned the assembled GIs before they had left: 'At the first sign of disobedience, my men will have not the slightest compunction in mowing you down. If it's their life or yours, *you will lose yours*! Please understand that.' And they understood well enough. The ruthless faces of the SS toughs watching them, vicious and hardened by five years of war, were sufficient proof that Krass was not joking. His Ascension Day Commando would shoot first and ask questions afterwards. Thus, as they retraced the route they had taken what seemed ages ago, Hardt racked his brain. But to no avail. He simply could not find a way out.

Just as the first dirty white light of the false dawn began to flush the night sky to the east, they started to approach their own lines. Beyond the six-wheel bulk of the buttoned-down Staghound, Hardt could make out the jagged lines of concertina wire and the squat irregular outlines of the foxholes. At the rear of the half-track, Krass, who had seen them too, tensed. 'All right, driver,' he rapped suddenly, 'swing by the armoured car and take up point?'

'Aw go and crap in yer cap!' Wheels snarled and for a moment the little yellow-faced ex-cabbie seemed about to refuse to obey the SS officer's command.

But Hardt had heard the click as Krass snapped off his safety catch and knew that the German would not hesitate to shoot. 'Okay, Wheels,' he grunted unhappily, 'knock it off. Do as the Kraut bastard says.'

Wheels put his foot down on the big accelerator angrily. The half-track shuddered and shot forward. It swung by the Staghound with only inches to spare and took up the lead position. 'Good,' Krass said approvingly. 'Now slow down again or you're liable to get yourself shot by your own people!'

Wheels cursed and released the pressure of his foot on the gas pedal. Before them the crew could make out the helmeted outlines of the defenders of the first line as they rose cautiously from their foxholes.

'Who goes there?' a thick Southern voice asked and there was no mistaking the tension in it at the sight of this American convoy appearing suddenly out of nowhere. 'I say — who goes there?'

Krass sprang forward and jammed his pistol into the small of Hardt's back. 'Answer!' he rasped.

The Major jerked into action. 'Friend,' he croaked. 'T-Force, Third Army.'

'Advance — *slowly* — and be recognised,' the soldier answered cautiously.

Even above the rattle of the half-track, Hardt could hear the metallic click of a machine gun bolt being drawn back cautiously. 'Okay, Wheels,' he ordered, his voice not quite under control, 'take her forward — nice and careful.'

With a curse, Wheels crashed home first gear and started to move forward at a snail's pace, while the rest of the convoy came to a halt behind them. But although he did not look back, Hardt was quite sure that the Staghound's cannon was keeping pace with their progress, ready to blow them to pieces at the first sign of treachery.

'Okay,' the Southern voice commanded, 'that's far enough. Hold it there, buddy!'

A tall slim figure detached itself from the shadows around the foxhole and came slowly and a little fearfully towards them, carbine at the ready. Then, as the soldier recognised the American uniforms inside the half-track, he lowered his weapon and said, 'Can't be too sure down on this section of the line, Major, the Krauts are a cunning lot of mothers!'

'Yes, quite right, soldier,' Krass answered in his flawless English before Hardt could reply, 'quite right.' Then he was businesslike again. 'What's the road to Bronvaux like?'

'Shit,' the sentry answered easily, 'as easy as walking ya best girl home. Not a Kraut within a mile and no potholes to speak of, Captain, sir.'

'Thank you, soldier.' He bent to Wheels, 'All right driver, you can take her away —'

'Just one moment, Captain, sir.'

Hardt stiffened. Had the sentry suspected something? If he had, he would die in exactly thirty seconds, but his suspicions would ruin the whole bold Kraut operation.

'Yes, soldier?' Krass asked cautiously, bringing up his pistol under the cover of the half-track's dashboard.

'Well, Captain sir.' The soldier was suddenly hesitant, almost shy. 'Me and the boys here', he indicated the foxhole line behind him, 'was with Captain Kee when you guys went in… Well, there ain't many of us left now. But I'm mighty proud — and the fellers too — that we didn't do it for nuthing —'

'Get on with it, soldier,' Krass snapped, aware that the soldier presented no danger now.

'I only wanted to ask, Captain, sir,' the sentry said humbly, 'if you wouldn't mind shaking ma hand — on behalf of the guys and poor old Captain Kee.'

Now it was Krass's turn to hesitate. In the faint dawn light, Hardt could see the little muscles ripple up and down the side of his scarred face, and he could imagine how the SS officer, brought up on the Germanic theories of racial superiority must be finding this moment. At any other time the American Major would have found the little scene very piquant, but not now. All Hardt could feel was an overwhelming sense of despair that everything seemed to be working out right for the arrogant, supercilious SS Captain.

'Of course, soldier,' Krass said with fake heartiness. 'Put it there!' He stretched out his hand.

'Thank you, Captain, sir,' the man said jovially and seized the German's white hand with his own coal-black one. 'I appreciate it.' He flashed a big, white-toothed grin at the rest of Old Baldy's crew.

'And the best o' luck to the rest of you Joes.' He withdrew his hand. 'Okay, Captain, sir, take 'em away!'

Hardt nudged Wheels. As Krass wiped the hand the black soldier had shook on his jacket, with a look of absolute disgust and loathing on his face, the little convoy started to roll forward once more. Hardt slumped down in his seat, sick to the heart. They were through without trouble. *Now only a miracle could save General Patton.*

Krass ordered a halt on the heights above Verdun. Since they had successfully penetrated the American first line, he had made a wide detour behind the front to avoid being asked awkward questions by the units packed close to the besieged city. Travelling at a moderate speed — in order not to attract the attention of Third Army's MPs who were always on the lookout for anyone breaking the Army's speed limit of fifty mph (Krass even knew that detail) — he had directed the convoy through Briey, via the backroad leading through Eton, and on to Etain into the area occupied by second line troops, who would not be inclined to ask questions of American troops nearly twenty miles behind the line. Now, feeling completely secure, he allowed both his own men and their prisoners to eat in front of the great towering *Ossuaire*, which contained the bones of a hundred and twenty thousand French and German unknown soldiers, who had been killed on these grim heights in the winter of 1916.

Everywhere the battle-hardened SS men were busy cooking tins of hash over cans filled with earth soaked in gas, warming their frozen hands over the flickering blue flames while they waited, chattering and laughing, happily, obviously very complacent this cold November morning.

'Look, at the Jerry sods,' Limey commented gloomily, shovelling cold hash out of a C-ration can, 'they're gonna pee their knickers in a mo — they're so sodding pleased with themselves!'

'Yeah,' Triggerman snarled, his sallow, olive face pinched with cold and repressed fury, 'Boy, gimme a grease gun for thirty seconds — *ner, twenty*, and I set them Kraut bastards up for a nice bunch of wooden overcoats.'

'*Cool it*,' Dutchie cut in, as the one-eyed NCO who had shot the prisoners in the courtyard turned to stare at them, idly stuffing a slice of sausage into his big mouth from the blade of his GI combat knife. 'That Kraut over there'd whip the nuts off you as quick as saying Jack Robinson. He's a real bad bastard!'

While the men ate, Krass, obviously as pleased with himself as his men were, confident now that nothing could stop him carrying out his daring mission, briefed Hardt on what he was going to do next. 'I think you will agree, Major,' he lectured Hardt, 'that these second-line troops of yours — clerks and cooks and the like — will present no problem. If they are like what we call the 'rear line stallion', they will be too occupied with lining their pockets on the black market and indulging themselves with the French mares.' He could not quite resist a sneer at that. 'God, how they can touch such things is beyond me! But no matter. Now I feel we can speed up our progress.'

'What do you mean?' Hardt asked, shivering a little, as his eyes took in the heaps of bones — skulls, legs, arms thrown together in hopeless confusion — through one of the porthole windows which lined the *Ossuaire*. Somehow the grim spectres of the futility of that ancient battle seemed to symbolise his own helpless position.

'I shall swing round Verdun, take the secondary road to Tours. I'll avoid Tours because our Intelligence tells us that you have a large number of troops stationed there, coming into Nancy just after dusk. Again Intelligence tells us that your famous General Patton likes to keep American office hours. He will be on his way to his quarters in that villa of his by five.' He smiled glacially at the look of utter dismay on Hardt's face.

'Yes, my dear Major, this operation is exceedingly well planned. We have thought of —'

'*Halt!*' Krass broke off suddenly as the cry of alarm rang out behind him. He swung round and took in the scene in a flash. One of the T-Force young replacements had kicked over a tin full of burning gas, scattering the SS men all around it and was running desperately for the cover of the autumn-bare trees beyond the *Ossuaire*. Behind him a couple of SS men, running all out, were unslinging their Schmeissers ready to cut him down the next instant.

Hastily Krass cupped his hands around his mouth. '*Don't shoot!*' he bellowed. 'Do you hear, men — don't shoot! I need him alive! Now catch him!'

The two SS troopers needed no urging. The Captain's bellowed order lent speed to their feet. Rapidly they closed on the bare-headed young soldier. He veered to the right, desperately trying to reach the cover of the trees. But the leading trooper out-thought him. Abruptly he whirled his Schmeisser around his head as if it were a cowboy's lasso and hurled it through the air with all his strength. The machine pistol caught the fugitive between his legs. He faltered. Hands gripped to wet sweating claws, Hardt prayed that he would remain upright. But that wasn't to be. The next instant he sprawled full length on the cold grass and the two SS men had flung themselves upon him and were pummelling him with their fists.

'So, you thought you would take French leave from us,' Krass said with fake pleasantness. 'Obviously you didn't like our company, eh?'

The tousled teenaged replacement hung his head, the blood dripping from his nose where the two troopers had punched him. He did not say a word. But his face was expressive enough; it proclaimed utter defeat. Hardt felt for him. But he dare not speak. Krass's mood was dangerous, highly dangerous, and he didn't want to do anything that might force violent action. Soon, he would realise that his concern had been of no avail.

Krass took his gaze off the replacement and looked at the stony-faced T-Force men, hemmed in on all sides by the Ascension Day Commando. 'This man thought he could escape. But as you see he was wrong,' he announced in his icy voice. 'Now as an object lesson to you all that I am not to be trifled with, I'm going to ensure that he will never do any running again. Held!'

'*Zu Befehl, Sturmbannführer!*' The evil-looking NCO, from whose empty eye socket a thin red liquid oozed, sprang to attention in front of the officer.

'See our young friend does not use his long legs again,' Krass commanded in German and pulling out his ivory cigarette holder, placed one of the sweet-perfumed Turkish cigarettes into it casually.

Held did not hesitate. 'You — and you,' he ordered. 'Grab hold of the *Ami!*'

Two of the watching troopers grabbed the replacement's arms. 'Hey, what's going on —' he began in alarm and then stopped as he saw the NCO commence to draw his pistol, his face suddenly ashen.

Big Red understood immediately what Held was going to do. 'You sadistic bastard!' he blurted out, his face crimson. Abruptly he dived forward out of the ranks of the prisoners. But he didn't get far. An SS man wolfing down the contents of a can of hot Spam thrust out his foot. Red went flying with a curse of rage. Next instant a rifle butt slammed down on the back of his big head and he went out like a light. A moment later Held took aim and fired.

At that range he could not miss. The boy's knee-cap shattered audibly. He screamed and fell to the ground, blood spurting a bright red through his fingers, tightly clenched around his ruined knee. But Held was not yet finished. Licking his lips pleasurably, he aimed and fired again. The boy screamed pitifully, his arms fanning the air, his second knee-cap smashed, crippled for life — if he managed to survive the loss of blood and the terrible shock of his mutilations.

Krass breathed out a ring of blue smoke. '*Danke, Held,*' he said, and then in English, 'All right, you can take him.' Casually he waved his elegantly manicured hand at the boy sprawled out in the damp grass, 'that is if you want him.'

As some of the boy's buddies ran forward to pick him up, Hardt looked at the German officer, his eyes burning with unbearable hate, and spat: 'Damn you, Krass, come what may, I'm gonna kill you, you bastard — *slowly!*'

Krass laughed. 'I doubt it, Major. I doubt it very greatly,' was his sole reply.

CHAPTER 4

'Gentlemen,' Patton announced solemnly to his assembled staff and Generals Eddy and Grow, 'we will attack Fort Driant once more tomorrow morning. I have made my decision, in spite of the goddam rain.'

There was an excited buzz of chatter among the staff. The tall grey-haired Army Commander smiled, showing his dingy, sawn-off teeth. It was the reaction he had anticipated.

But there was no smile on General Eddy's round, bespectacled face; only a worried frown. 'But General,' he objected, 'you can't expect my corps to attack in this weather, which is forecast to continue! Air support will be nil, you know that. And my divisions are tired, General.'

Patton's smile vanished. He looked at XII Corps' Commander severely, 'There are no tired divisions, only tired commanders, Eddy,' he said coldly to the man who had served under him since North Africa.

'That may be, General,' Eddy answered, his face flushing an even deeper red. 'But that rain out there'll make the conditions hell for my boys.'

'I agree with General Eddy, sir,' Grow, Commander of Eddy's lead armoured division, joined in.

Patton gave the two general officers the benefit of his frightening Number Three Frown, while his staff waited for the explosion to come. But instead of exploding into his usual colourful invective, Patton asked quietly, 'You feel that under present conditions you cannot undertake the attack as planned?'

'That is correct,' the other two answered in unison.

'Would you care to make recommendations as to your successors?'

There was a sudden heavy silence in the big ops room that dominated his Nancy HQ in the *Rue du Sergent Blandau*. For what seemed an age, the brass stood frozen into their stances. Then Patton said, his voice warm and encouraging again. 'Come on over to the map, Eddy and I'll tell you what I'm gonna do.'

For the next twenty minutes he pumped the two officers' drained reservoirs of self-confidence full of the elixir of his own vitality and determination. 'So you see, gentlemen,' he concluded, 'you don't need to worry, I have reason to believe that my T-Force has already knocked out those Kraut batteries — or at least some of them — covering Driant. If you can get your doughs within striking distance of the Fort, you won't need to worry about those Kraut guns.' He smiled. 'Now I want you to go back to your Headquarters, have a big drink and get some darn sleep.'

'Don't worry, General,' Eddy said, a new confidence in his voice at Patton's revelation about the Führer Battery, 'the attack will go on.'

Patton nodded. 'You're goddam right it will.'

But when the two rebellious Generals had departed, Patton's confident look disappeared and his watching staff noted the worried frown which pinched his lean face. Suddenly he looked old, very old.

Colonel Codman picked up the Army Commander's gleaming lacquered helmet and proffered it in silence. Patton accepted it and said despondently, 'You know, Charley, I think this has been the longest goddam day of the war for me.'

Codman, his senior aide, nodded his understanding. The General's mood now was as dreary and depressed as the wet evening.

'I can believe that, sir,' he said softly. 'But I'm afraid there's more to come this evening.'

Patton nodded as his staff stiffened to the position of attention. 'Yeah, you can say that again, Charley.' Wearily he touched his hand to his helmet in salute. 'Okay, Charley let's get back to the Rue Auxerre and get on with this farce.'

In silence the two of them strode out of the ops room towards the waiting staff car.

The blackout had already draped Nancy in heavy darkness as they began to move into the big Lorraine city. The only lights now were those of the US trucks rumbling towards the front to the north and the torches of whores soliciting business from GIs in the big eighteenth century doorways. Gloomily Hardt told himself no one would stop them at this time of night and in this kind of weather.

Despondently he hunched in his seat, the rain dripping miserably from the rim of his helmet, while a confident Krass gave Wheels direction after direction, in such a manner that Hardt hated him solely on account of his perfection. They hissed down the Quai Claude de Lorraine and turned off towards Nancy's Place Stanislas. The famous square was empty, save for a few street-walkers, their macs gleaming in the rain, as the convoys' lights picked them out for an instant. The city, or so it seemed to Hardt, despairing that nothing would ever be able to stop the arrogant SS officer now, had gone to bed for the night.

Krass, his scarred face hollowed out to a death's head by the faint glow of the controls, seemed to be able to read Hardt's thoughts. 'Yes, my dear Major, I'm afraid you've lost. Nancy has gone to bed with chickens. There is no one about to stop us now.' He was businesslike again. 'All right, driver, turn off left here and keep straight on till you come to the next fork, then bear right at the *Rue Saint Nicolas*.'

Wheels cursed under his breath but did as he was told. The little object lesson with the young replacement at the Verdun Ossuary had had its effect. They sped on.

Hardt breathed out hard and wondered for a moment what kind of a crime this paragon of military virtue and leadership must have committed to have been posted to a punishment outfit. It must have been pretty awful.

More slowly now, with Old Baldy in the lead once more, they left the *Cours Leopold* behind and began to roll over the slippery *pavé* towards the suburb of Maxeville. Hardt shook his head, half in dismay, half in admiration. Krass had swung round the city twice, obviously making quite sure that he wasn't walking into some sort of trap. But ne had nothing to fear on that score. The residential suburb was absolutely silent, wrapped up heavily in the blackout, the only sound, the echo of their own motors as they rumbled down the narrow streets. Luck seemed to be on the Kraut bastard's side all the way.

They rolled by the big brewery which dominated the area and began to climb up towards the high ground, the spiked silhouette of a fir wood dominating it. 'All right,' Krass whispered, as if the enemy could hear his words, 'driver, take her a little slower now.'

Wheels obliged. Now the half-track was crawling along between seventeenth century villas, carefully blacked-out and almost hidden behind high crumbling stone walls. The men in the half-track tensed, they could hear music, and it was music familiar to all of them.

'Glen Miller!' van Fleet exclaimed.

'Yes, that's right,' Krass agreed, 'Major Glenn Miller's famous Eighth Air Force Band. Funny people you Americans, making a purveyor of decadent black music an officer!'

Inside Hardt groaned. The German bastard seemed to know everything! But he had no time to dwell on Krass's seeming infallibility, for the SS officer had suddenly gripped Wheels' shoulder hard and was ordering him to stop. Savagely Wheels braked and the half-track shook with the violence of his sudden stop. One after the other, vehicles halted behind them, their motors ticking over softly.

Held appeared out of the gloom, Schmeisser at the ready. 'Watch them,' Krass snapped. 'You,' he spoke to the two troopers who had held the fugitive while the evil-looking NCO had shot him through the knees, 'come with me. And you, Major Hardt, you come too.'

Hardt hesitated.

Hastily Krass screwed a long clumsy-looking object, which the Major recognised as a silencer, on to the end of his pistol and thrust it savagely into the American's ribs. 'I'd advise you to move *now!*' he hissed.

'He means it, skipper,' van Fleet said urgently. 'You'd better go with him.'

Hardt cursed and rose to his feet, as to their rear the Staghounds' electrically operated turrets swung round noiselessly to bring their guns to bear on the cowed, silent Americans.

Cautiously the four of them began to move towards the villa, which housed General Patton and his entourage, almost hidden from the street by a high wall. Noiselessly they worked their way along the shadows cast by the wall until Krass commanded suddenly, '*Halt!*'

They stopped and Hardt could see now where the music was coming from. Two white-helmeted MPs were huddled in their gleaming wet coats against the red and white striped pole which barred the entrance to Patton's quarters, listening to a small portable radio propped up inside a dimly lit sentry box.

'They would be shot for such carelessness in the Armed SS,' Krass sneered. 'But no matter. We will let them live for a little while longer. After all, their carelessness serves our purpose, doesn't it?' He rapped out something in German and the two troopers bent stiffly. Krass put his right foot in their cupped hands. 'Now!' he commanded. With a grunt they heaved him up on to the top of the wall. 'Now you, Hardt,' he said.

A few moments later the four of them were over the wall, the slight noise they made drowned by the Glen Miller band launching into *Little Brown Jug*. Carefully they began to work their way out of the thick wet shrubs which lined the inside of the wall, towards the big house, with Krass in the lead and Hardt following, urged on by the two tense SS troopers.

Now they could see that General Patton's blackout was not altogether perfect. His elderly black servant Sergeant George Meeks must have slipped up that night, for there was a chink of yellow light coming from one of the tall French windows. Krass crept over to it, attracted by both the light and the soft hum of many voices coming from within. Hastily the others followed, making no sound as they sped through the wet grass.

Krass pressed his eye against the dripping window, the rain running down the back of his gleaming helmet. '*Grossartig!*' he muttered triumphantly to himself and then to Hardt. 'Take a look, Major. There he is — your famous General Patton and his happy band. Just as we planned.'

Hardt peered through the gap in the curtains. Krass was right. Patton, looking old and tired, was sitting at the head of the gleaming white table, toying with a glass of red wine, while at his feet his fat overfed pooch, Willie, gnawed at a bone. Seated on both sides, mostly preoccupied with their food, their conversation as black as that of their chief, were his staff officers, Harkins, Koch, Gay. He recognised half a dozen of them, as they pecked at their food, and realised that the whole Third Army would be paralysed if Krass succeeded in assassinating them as well as Patton. New army commanders might well be found after a couple of days, but it took months to train officers of the calibre of the men sitting at the long table, who knew the working of the three hundred thousand-man strong Third in and out.

Krass dug his fingers into Hardt's arm cruelly. 'Come on, Major, you've seen enough of them. We've got to get back to the others.' He chuckled softly, an uncanny sound at that particular moment. 'I think it would be only fair to allow them to enjoy their Last Supper, don't you?'

Moments later they were running through the sheeting rain back the way they had come. Now, if Krass's plan worked, General George S. Patton had only a matter of minutes left to live.

CHAPTER 5

Swiftly Krass made his dispositions as the rain hurtled down in a solid sheet, striking the war-torn earth with a vicious, never-ending hiss, as if it would have liked nothing better than to wash it away for good. As far as Hardt could make out from Krass's rapid, clipped Northern German, the SS officer's plan was simple but highly effective.

One Staghound would remain outside the complex on the street, covering the entrance and the remaining T-Force men, huddled together in cold, soaking misery in the open jeeps. Meanwhile the one-eyed NCO, Held, would go over the wall with a couple of troopers armed with Spandaus, to come up at the rear of the Patton villa and prevent anyone escaping from a back door or window. In the meantime Old Baldy and the other Staghound would pass through the sentries at the gate, feigning an urgent message for the Third Army commander. Once everyone was in position, the Staghound and the half-track would start blasting all hell out of the dining room with their combined cannon and half-inch machine guns. As Krass assured them: at point blank range like that, they simply couldn't miss killing the 'cowboy General and those fat-arsed rear echelon stallions he calls a staff!'

When he had finished, Krass looked round the circle of hardened, rain-swept faces, brutalised by three years of the most terrible combat in the Russian wastes, and said emotionally, 'SS men, comrades, I know you won't let me down, whatever happens. You see when we have completed this mission, our honour will have been restored and we will be allowed to return to our parent units. General Priess personally promised me that on his word as an SS officer.' He paused momentarily and in the faint green glow that came from the instruments on Old Baldy's dash, Hardt could catch a glimpse of Krass's face. It was suddenly very soft, the hard lines vanished, his eyes unnaturally excited — almost sexually so — as he gazed at the tough masculine features all around him. It was filled with a vaguely feminine longing and abruptly Hardt knew, with a sense of disgust, why Krass had been posted to the Ascension Day Commando. As a young man at the Point he had seen enough faces like that, hanging around the hamburger havens and drug stores frequented by the straight, clean-limbed teenage cadets from the Academy, their eyes filled with strange longing. *Sturmbannführer* Krass was queer!

Then the look had vanished as swiftly as it had come and Krass was rasping sotto voce, '*Kamaraden, Sieg Heil.*'

The SS troopers clicked their heels together, their hollowed out, fanatical faces raised to the pelting rain, '*Sieg Heil, Sturmbannführer!*' they hissed.

Krauss turned to Hardt as his men moved away to their positions. 'You'll live,' he said, 'if you do exactly as I say. But one foot wrong and you're as good as dead already. Clear?'

Hardt did not believe one word he said. As soon as the op was over, Krass would kill the lot of them. He had no illusions about that. He would not leave anyone behind who might blab how he had penetrated the American lines and how, presumably, he intended to return to the besieged city. 'I see,' he said carefully, forcing himself to keep his voice neutral, knowing that he would have to do something — *anything* — in the next five minutes if he were to prevent a tragedy of monumental proportions. 'What are your orders, Krass?'

Slowly, at the prescribed ten kilometres per hour ordered by the signs on both sides of the approach road, the half-track and the buttoned-down Staghound rattled up to the gate of Patton's HQ, making enough noise, even above the hiss of the rain, to alert the two white-helmeted MPs. The bigger of the two — a Corporal — flashed his torch and the half-track shuddered to a stop obediently enough. The Corporal stepped close to the half-track, his helmet and long black rubber slicker gleaming in the rain. 'What do you guys want here?' he asked, apparently in no way surprised by the appearance of two armoured vehicles at this time of the night.

Krass dug his pistol into the small of Hardt's back menacingly. At this late stage of the operation he was taking no chances that his own English might give him away. 'Tell him,' he hissed.

'T-Force, Corporal,' Hardt said thickly, thinking of his men outside who would be massacred if he slipped up. 'We've got an urgent message for General Patton — *a very important message*, you understand,' he said the words with unnecessary, un-American emphasis, desperately willing the Corporal to look at his face and recognise the frantic look of alarm and warning in his eyes. But nothing of the sort happened. The Corporal refused to raise his gaze. He kept his helmeted head bent in dull refusal, as if he were mesmerised by the persistent downpour. 'Okay, take a right,' he grunted. 'First building on the left. The General's still eating chow. You'd better ask for the OD. On your way.'

Almost before Hardt, utterly downcast, realised what was happening, the other MP had raised the red-and-white striped barrier, Wheels had rammed home first gear, and they were rattling through into the grounds. He had failed again.

Slowly, inevitably, the two vehicles drew closer and closer to the General's villa, guided through the streaming darkness by that yellow chink of light which escaped from between the thick drapes like a beacon. Hardt was paralysed — all decision, energy drained from his body. It was like in a bad dream when one was absolutely powerless to avert the overwhelming catastrophe which one knew was approaching. As if turned to stone, he sat rooted to his seat and let it happen.

Krass nudged Wheels. 'All right,' he ordered, his voice thick and tense with excitement, 'stop now.'

The half-track came to a halt. Behind them the Staghound did the same. 'Watch them,' Krass snapped to the SS man he had brought with him. He scrambled through the sullen crew of Old Baldy and pushed Limey away from his place behind, the red glowing radio. Hastily he slipped on the earphones and called the buttoned-down armoured car, its gun turning noiselessly to point at the villa. 'Thirty seconds from — *now*,' he rasped and clicked off the set. He looked up, his cruel face glowing with excited triumph. '*Sturmman, an das Gewehr!*' he ordered.

The SS man jumped to the heavy .5 machine gun located to the right of the driver's seat. Expertly, he drew back the bolt and rammed it home again. Standing there with his weapon pointed at the nearest French window, he waited for the order to open fire. And still Hardt seemed unable to move. Behind them, Krass counted off the seconds, his lips moving soundlessly. *Twenty … fifteen … ten…*

But suddenly all hell was let loose! On the roof the soaked, frozen lookout who had been observing the convoy ever since it had first entered the steep cobbled street, lugged the pin out of the phosphorus grenade and dropped it over the side. It exploded with a soft plop. Abruptly night was turned to day, as it threw out a blinding white, incandescent light. It was the signal the HQ troops had been waiting for.

The bazooka man posted in the sentry box pushed aside the portable radio. *Little Brown Jug* came to a sudden stop. Crouching there in the pelting rain, he aimed and fired at the Staghound in the same instant. At that close range he could not miss. The six-wheeled armoured car reared up in the air like a wild horse being saddled for the first time. Next instant it crashed down, vicious blue flames shooting up from its shattered gas tank, and the big MP Corporal was spraying the stricken vehicle with his grease gun, shouting wildly at the same time, '*T-Force, get outa them jeeps ... outa them jeeps — at the double!* Move *it!*'

For one long moment, neither the SS men nor Old Baldy's crew could take in what was happening. Bathed in the glowing flickering white light of the grenade, they crouched there frozen in melodramatic poses like characters in a third-rate play. But when the front door to the villa flew open to reveal Patton himself, twin ivory-handled pistols in his hands, big cigar jutting out of his pugnacious mouth, flanked by a group of heavily armed aides, they woke up to what was happening.

'*Don't sit there, like a fart in a trance, Red!*' Limey yelled urgently at the big NCO in the front of the halftrack, '*Get that gunner!*'

Red shot out one of his big paws, just as the gunner was about to press the trigger. The .5 tilted to the dripping sky. White ana red tracer zig-zagged harmlessly into nothing. Next instant the SS man was thrust against the windshield and Red was pounding him mercilessly with his ham like fists. Limey grabbed for the officer next to the radio. Krass dodged and whipped the barrel of his pistol across the little Cockney's face. He yelped with pain and staggered back, his nose broken. The bazooka team, stalking the second Staghound, launched their rocket at point blank range. Its impact sent the armoured car swaying from side to side, as if caught in a violent storm. Krass dropped over the side and darted away into the glowing darkness to their right. 'After him!' Hardt yelled, waking out of his trance at last, 'Don't let the bastard get away!'

The crew of Old Baldy needed no urging. They all had a score to settle with *Sturmbannführer* Krass. Leaving the bleeding SS gunner to slump back on to the metal floor unconscious, Big Red dropped over the side, followed an instant later by the rest. Behind them the Staghound's gun drooped like the head of a dying animal. Its magazine exploded. Great glowing shards of metal hissed murderously through the air. In the villa the windows shattered. The blast whipping his uniform about his lean frame, Patton ducked hastily and yelled in his high-pitched voice, 'Get those goddam heads down, men!'

But the Old Baldy crew did not heed the explosion. They were intent on the running man vanishing into the darkness in front of them. 'He's trying to team up with the other bastard at the back!' van Fleet cried.

A moment later the chatter of a BAR followed by the swifter, high-pitched hysterical burr of a Schmeisser told them that Held was already being engaged by the HQ Company which had sprung the trap on the SS Commando. Krass must have realised that escape in that direction was impossible too, for in that very same instant his pursuers heard a crash of glass as if the fugitive had put his booted foot through a window.

'He's trying to get into the house,' Hardt yelled urgently. 'This way!'

They pelted round a corner. A French window hung open, drapes torn aside, the yellow light from the chandeliers streaming out into the wet darkness. 'He's in there, sir!' Big Red gasped and crunched over the shattered glass into the big empty room. The others ran after him, clattering through the operations room, scattering raindrops on both sides.

'He's up here!' Red, in the lead, cried.

They swung out of the room and came to a sudden stop. Krass, his face blanched with fear, was poised on the great staircase above. Below Patton, crouched like a gun-slinger, pistols in hands, flanked by his tense-faced staff officers, was staring up at him as if hypnotised. 'Come on, you bastard, drop that gun,' he commanded.

Krass came to life abruptly. Almost, as if he were not aware himself what he was doing, he squeezed the trigger of his pistol. The explosive bullet, with which he had loaded it just before the assassination attempt, hit one of Patton's staff squarely in the face. It disappeared in a ball of red flame. Blood and shattered bone splattered everywhere. The staff officer slammed against the nearest wall, leaving what was left of his shattered head on the carpet at Patton's feet.

'*Scatter*!' Patton cried at the top of his voice. The elegant staff officers flung themselves on the ground everywhere.

Codman dived at the General's feet and dragged him down too, cursing and stuttering with impotent fury, still desperately trying to aim his ivory-handled revolvers, as another explosive bullet hissed through the air just above his head and shattered in the woodwork, showering them with splinters and plaster.

In that same instant, van Fleet's second knife hissed through the air. His aim was off, but the blade caught Krass in the right arm instead of the heart. But it sufficed. He howled piteously and the big pistol clattered to the stairs. They had him at last!

Krass backed away as they formed a semi-circle around him, no sound save their harsh breathing. Like a trapped animal his eyes darted back and forth, taking in their hard, set faces, trying to find some way of escape and finding none. The T-Force men came closer.

Below, the staff were beginning to rise to their feet. 'What the Sam Hill's going on up there?' Patton's voice demanded angrily, as Codman helped him up.

None of them answered. Now they heard nothing, saw nothing but their victim. Krass knew suddenly what they were going to do to him. '*Nein*,' he screamed, his English forgotten now. '*Bitte nicht* —'

His words ended in a hysterical, feminine scream as Big Red kneed him cruelly. Krass sank to one knee, clutching his ruined testicles, vomit spilling from his gasping mouth.

'Sweet Jesus, forgive me!' Dutchie Schulze breathed fervently and rammed the heel of his muddy combat boot into Krass's sweat-lathered face. He screamed thickly through the vomit and slammed against the wall, bright blood spurting up from his shattered nose and mouth.

The blood seemed to act like a signal. As one they fell upon him. Something snapped. The resentments, the heartbreak, the cruelties of the last few days in captivity welled to the surface, as bitter as green bile. For a few moments they became animals, overcome by a burning atavistic fury, mouthing obscenities, slamming their boots over and over again into the writhing, twisting screaming man on the floor, while Patton cried fervently, '*Stop it! Stop it, I say!… My God Almighty, they're slaughtering that Kraut…*'

But they didn't hear. They continued their murderous work, eyes gleaming crazily, grunting with pleasure almost, as the battered, unrecognisable thing on the floor twitched one last time and then lay motionless, the boots which thudded into its broken ribs no longer having any effect. And then finally it was over. The staff officers were pushing T-Force savagely to one side, crying over and over again, '*Stop it willya, you crazy bums!*' Trying to get them away from the bloody mess on the floor which had once been *Sturmbannführer* Krass. And they were swaying from side to side like drunken men, blinking their eyes, as if they could not believe what they had been capable of doing...

PART FIVE: D-DAY AT DRIANT

'Well, Hardt, T-Force pulled it off once again… So, after this, Germany and then — who knows? One thing is certain though, whatever happens there. I'll be needing you guys of T-Force. That's for goddam sure!'

Gen. George Patton to Major Hardt, November 8th, 1944.

CHAPTER 1

General Patton, dressed in full uniform save for his riding boots and lacquered helmet, awoke at three o'clock on the morning of November 8th, 1944. Even before he had padded in his stockinged feet to the window, drawn back the blackout drapes and peered out into the darkness, he knew, with a sinking feeling, that his prayers of the previous evening had not been answered. It was still raining, as hard as ever, as if it would never goddamwell stop!

Slowly he crawled back to his warm bed, shivering a little with the cold. But he could not sleep; he was too jittery about the morning's attack. Instead he picked up Rommel's book, *Infantry Attacks*, from the night table and by chance opened the well-thumbed book at the page where Rommel (now dead these many weeks by his own hand at Hitler's express order) described the heavy rains of September 1914 and how the old Imperial German Army struggling through France still managed despite the weather. A little comforted he read a further half hour and fell asleep again over the book.

He awoke at 5:15 precisely. For a moment he lay there puzzled by the great roar. Then he realised what it was — the preliminary barrage, tearing the pre-dawn stillness apart with a malignant, elemental fury. The softening-up for the attack had commenced. 'His will be done!' he muttered quietly to himself and, rising hastily, started to pull on his gleaming riding boots.

Together with his staff, slow and thick-mouthed at this time of the morning, he stepped out, past the burnt-out armoured car, to watch the spectacle, a slicker wrapped loosely around his shoulders against the rain. Above them a few brave stars twinkled in a dark, damp sky, but to the east the whole horizon flickered and trembled a blood red with the impact of four hundred guns.

Patton licked his dry lips. Now he knew his whole front was on the move. The 90th Infantry Division would be moving into its assault boats to make a surprise crossing of the Moselle, while his 10th Armoured's Shermans would be grinding north through the mud to just behind the covering infantry point. Now everything depended upon the capture of Fort Driant, so that it could not wipe out his doughs massing to cross the Moselle. But had Hardt's T-Force destroyed the right guns at the Führer Battery? That was the overwhelming question: *would the Führer Battery remain silent?*

At eight o'clock, with the weather still too bad for TAC Air to come to his aid, General Bradley, his superior, called. 'What are your plans, Georgie?' he asked without preliminaries.

'I'm attacking, Brad,' Patton answered, looking smug. 'Can't you hear the guns?'

'What! You're attacking without air support, Georgie!' Then the Army Group Commander caught himself. 'Splendid, Georgie,' he enthused, while Patton told himself that as usual his boss would catch on to his coat-tails and try to claim the credit for the new offensive now that the front was moving again at last. 'Hang on, Georgie, Ike is here and wants to speak to you.'

'Georgie,' Patton recognised Eisenhower's familiar voice, now silkier than ever and he pulled a wry face. Like Bradley, Ike was another headquarters General — 'canteen commandos', he called them — whose sole function was, or so it seemed, to stop him from getting on with the real shooting war. 'This is Ike — your Supreme Commander, you know. I'm thrilled, boy! I expect a hell of a lot from you, so carry the ball all the way.'

'Thanks, General,' Patton answered stiffly. 'We will, sir, we sure will!'

But as he put the field telephone down and prepared to go up front, that nagging question was still uppermost in his mind, belying the confidence of his answer to Eisenhower: *would the Führer Battery remain silent?*

In spite of the rain, Patton and his aide Codman drove to Driant in an open jeep. 'Who the Sam Hill is worried about a few spots of rain, I'm not *that* old, Codman! I want my doughs to see me and know the Old Man is right up there at the front with them!'

Behind the jeep, Old Baldy rattled along in the place of honour before the olive drab staff cars. 'Jesus,' Patton had growled to Codman when he had protested, 'if those guys could go into that hell's kitchen and risk their lives for me, the least I can do, Charley, is to put my life in their hands. T-Force will be my bodyguard this day!' Thus the Tommy gun toting bodyguard, who usually rode next to the Commanding General, were relegated to the last truck, in which travelled the two scruffy French civilians who had sneaked out of Metz thirty-six hours before to bring the vital warning to Patton's HQ.

The crew of Old Baldy rode in silence, even the usual ebullient Limey spoke little, but perhaps that was due to the pain from his nose, covered by an enormous plaster so that he looked, as Triggerman had snarled after the MO had finished with the little Cockney, 'like a pissy-assed parrot, with that snoot!'

Moodily, already visualising to themselves what would happen if they had failed in their mission, they took in the signs of the big push on both sides of the road — the line of box-like ambulances, with the sign CARRYING CASUALTIES already propped in their windshields, their drivers smoking and waiting for what was to come; heavy bridging equipment and motor boats, complete with blue uniformed sailors from the Fleet looking completely out of place in this sea of khaki; row after row of Shermans, glistening in the rain, with the usual battalion comic, clad in a looted top hat and carrying a tattered umbrella, play-acting in front of his tense comrades; and the infantry, heads already bowed under the weight of their equipment, as if in defeat, plodding on steadily through the mud of the verges, moving up to their own particular date with destiny.

The roar of the guns grew louder. They swung round a bend in the road and then they were there. Towering up above the waiting infantry crouched in their muddy holes, up to their knees in water, the shape of Fort Driant, already shrouded a little in yellow smoke, stood there, doggedly defiant, as if challenging them to try once again — at their peril.

As the convoy came to a halt to let officers descend before the drivers scuttled away with their vehicles to the shelter of a nearby gully, the infantry, waiting in their trenches, turned to stare at them. A buck sergeant whistled through his front teeth and exclaimed, 'Gee, just look who blew in, guys, *ole Blood an' Guts hissen!*'

'Yeah, his guts — and our blood,' the company wag said but nobody took any notice of him. They were too fascinated by the sight of the immaculately turned out Army Commander, who strode purposefully to the height from which he would observe the attack on Fort Driant like the God of War personally.

Ten minutes later, just as the attack was about to kick off, there was a faint buzz from the west which grew louder by the second; and then abruptly the rain stopped, the sun was shining a weak yellow, and the sky was full of fighter bombers, hundreds of them, streaking towards their targets like silver arrows, criss-crossed by vapour trails and the curling smoke spirals of the pathfinders' markers.

Patton's eyes lit up at once. 'What do you say to that, Hardt?' he exclaimed enthusiastically. 'The flyboys came after all — and in this goddam weather. Hot shit, I'm almost sorry for those Kraut bastards up there!'

'Yessir,' Hardt said, not sharing the General's enthusiasm, as the first dive-bomber fell out of the sky and hurtled towards the Fort at four hundred mph. All the dive-bombers in the world wouldn't knock Driant out. The crunch would come once they had stopped and the infantry began advancing up that long, barren slope. 'Start praying, Clarry,' he yelled above the roar of the first explosion, 'like you've never prayed before that we knocked the right darned cannon out!'

Van Fleet nodded glumly. 'Yeah, you can say that again, skipper!'

Slowly the smoke of the aerial bombardment began to drift away. On the hill the watchers tensed. This was it! Already the infantry officers down below were straightening up, blowing their whistles, adding their noise to the bellowed commands of the noncoms. The infantry began to move out, following the Shermans which were rumbling up the slope ahead. Almost at once the German mortars howled into action. The first tanks were hit, heeling from side to side as they were struck, churning to a sudden stop as their tracks snapped, burning fiercely with sailing ribbons of white smoke vanishing in the sky a hundred feet above them. But the GIs plodding doggedly up the slope, trying to keep their balance in the mud, seemed not to notice the din; their sole concern appeared to be the effort of lifting their boots, heavy with the muck which clung to them as if they were soled with lead.

The enemy machine guns opened up with a vicious whine. The infantry started to fall everywhere. 'Lord Jesus, receive their souls unto Thee,' Dutchie whispered behind Hardt, his big eyes full of horror, and began to mumble an anguished prayer. The infantry commenced to run heavily, angry with the mud, the Krauts, the war, the long siege of this remote French city, eager to vent their rage on the unseen enemy.

'Goddamn,' Patton yelled enthusiastically, 'they're gonna do it this time!'

Hardt tensed at his side. Soon they would know. Now the first GIs were clambering through the barbed wire. Behind them the combat engineers unslung the nozzles of their flame-throwers and pressed the triggers. Blue flaming liquid squirted towards the first enemy trenches. Suddenly the air — even at that distance — was heavy with the sweet stench of burned flesh. A handful of ragged, blackened Germans came stumbling out into the daylight, hands raised high in the air, to be sent stumbling down the slope with a kick in the rear.

'Attaboy!' Patton cried, beside himself with glee, as the lead infantry sprang over the captured trenches. A Sherman followed, trailing wire behind it. Instinctively a group of the GIs waited and formed up behind it. The tank driver hit the gas. The tracks showered the crouching soldiers with mud. But they stuck to their positions, as it began to climb the wall of the Fort.

Hardt felt the sweat begin to break out all over his body in spite of the November chill. His hands were clenched into wet claws. The Sherman was nearly on the top of the Fort now. Hardt willed it to make it. The next instant it had, and was rumbling towards the head of the nearest ventilation shaft, followed by a couple of GIs carrying long Bangalore torpedoes. While the GIs prepared their charges, the Sherman ground to a halt, its electrically operated turret swinging round menacingly, its long, hooded 75mm gun at the alert, ready to tackle anyone who wanted to stop the frantic activity of the two GIs. Hardt's eyes scanned the horizon desperately. But those blinking yellow lights which would signal the slaughter to follow were absent. In that same moment, the first Bangalore torpedo exploded with a thick muffled crump somewhere in the interior of the Fort, and the waiting infantry tensed to follow up the second explosion down into the shattered darkness.

Patton swung round, his pale blue eyes lit up like stars on a Christmas Tree. 'Hot shit, Hardt, you did it! You knocked the buggers out. Look at those doughs up there, *they're going in now*! Put it there!' He thrust out his hand and Hardt took it in a daze, hardly daring to believe the evidence of his own eyes. But it was no illusion. The Führer Battery was silent, as more and more GIs scuttled across the roof of the great fort and disappeared into the smoking interior like a colony of deadly ants. The fight for Fort Driant was not over by a long chalk, that he knew, but the presence of the GIs fighting their way through the Fort's dark stinking corridors would put an end to any danger that it could present to the 90th Infantry Division already streaming across the River Moselle on their way to Germany. The road ahead was free.

Five minutes later they had trooped back to the staff cars parked in the safety of the gully, leaving the battle of Fort Driant to the infantry; General Patton had many more units of his victorious advancing Third Army to visit this day. Just before he stepped into his jeep, Colonel Codman introduced Gallo to him and explained that the black-haired Frenchman was the man who had saved T-Force and probably his own life with the timely warning he had smuggled out of Metz. Patton shook the Political Commissar's hand warmly, expressing his thanks energetically in fluent if somewhat ungrammatical French, while Codman, a great Francophile, beamed at the two of them. But Patton's lean face darkened abruptly when Gallo cut short his flow of words with the cold statement that he had a request: he wanted to enter the city with the victorious American troops when it fell and take over the administration in 'the name of the workers and peasants, in the name of the French Communist Party!'

Hastily Patton bit back an angry retort, for he hated 'Reds' next to 'Krauts'. But he had reason to be grateful to the cold-eyed, dark-haired Commissar. 'I'll see what can be done Monsieur Gallo,' he said coldly. 'But you must remember that Metz has not been captured yet and there is many a slip between the cup and the lip.' And with that he dismissed the Frenchman.

'Well, Hardt,' he said thoughtfully, his eyes fixed on Gallo's leather-jacketed back, as Mims fumbled with the jeep's starter, 'T-Force pulled it off once again, eh?'

Hardt grunted something about how he could not fail with such men under his command.

But Patton was not really listening; he was preoccupied with his thoughts, his expression grim despite his victory at Fort Driant. As the jeep's engine roared into life, he said, 'So after this, Germany and then — who knows?' His voice rose with sudden determination, as if he could already visualise the new enemy to come. 'One thing is certain, though, whatever happens there, I'll be needing you guys of T-Force. That's for goddam sure!'

An instant later the jeep lurched forward, Mims sounding the General's 'steamboat trombone' horn at full blast, scattering tardy staff officers to left and right, heading towards the grey November horizon, with its fresh problems, its fresh battles, into an uncertain future...

A NOTE TO THE READER

Dear Reader,

If you have enjoyed this novel enough to leave a review on **Amazon** and **Goodreads**, then we would be truly grateful.

Sapere Books

Sapere Books is an exciting new publisher of brilliant fiction and popular history.

To find out more about our latest releases and our monthly bargain books visit our website:
saperebooks.com